Mark Rutherford, Reuben Shapcott

The Autobiography of Mark Rutherford

Mark Rutherford, Reuben Shapcott

The Autobiography of Mark Rutherford

ISBN/EAN: 9783337075064

Printed in Europe, USA, Canada, Australia, Japan

Cover: Foto ©Raphael Reischuk / pixelio.de

More available books at **www.hansebooks.com**

THE AUTOBIOGRAPHY

OF

MARK RUTHERFORD,

DISSENTING MINISTER.

EDITED BY HIS FRIEND,

REUBEN SHAPCOTT.

LONDON:

TRÜBNER & CO., LUDGATE HILL.

1881.

CONTENTS.

———o———

This is the night when I must die,
And great Orion walketh high
In silent glory overhead:
He'll set just after I am dead.

A week this night, I'm in my grave:
Orion walketh o'er the wave:
Down in the dark damp earth I lie,
While he doth march in majesty.

A few weeks hence and spring will come;
The earth will bright array put on
Of daisy and of primrose bright,
And everything which loves the light.

And some one to my child will say,
 " You'll soon forget that you could play
Beethoven; let us hear a strain
From that slow movement once again."

And so she'll play that melody,
While *I* among the worms do lie;
Dead to them all, for ever dead;
The churchyard clay dense overhead.

I once did think there might be mine
One friendship perfect and divine;
Alas! that dream dissolved in tears
Before *I*'d counted twenty years.

For *I* was ever commonplace;
Of genius never had a trace;
My thoughts the world have never fed,
Mere echoes of the book last read.

Those whom *I* knew *I* cannot blame:
If they are cold, *I* am the same:
How could they ever show to me
More than a common courtesy?

There is no deed which *I* have done;
There is no love which *I* have won,
To make them for a moment grieve
That *I* this night their earth must leave.

Thus, moaning at the break of day,
A man upon his deathbed lay;
A moment more and all was still;
The Morning Star came o'er the hill.

But when the dawn lay on his face,
It kindled an immortal grace;
As if in death that Life were shown
Which lives not in the great alone.

Orion sank down in the west
Just as he sank into his rest;
I closed in solitude his eyes,
And watched him till the sun's uprise.

AUTOBIOGRAPHY

OF

MARK RUTHERFORD.

——o——

CHAPTER I.

CHILDHOOD.

NOW that I have completed my autobiography up to the present year, I sometimes doubt whether it is right to publish it. Of what use is it, many persons will say, to present to the world what is mainly a record of weaknesses and failures? If I had any triumphs to tell; if I could show how I had risen superior to poverty and suffering; if, in short, I were a hero of any kind whatever, I might perhaps be justified in communicating my success to mankind, and stimulating them to do as I have done. But mine is the tale of a common-place life, perplexed by many problems I have never solved; disturbed by many difficulties I have never surmounted; and blotted by ignoble concessions which are a constant regret. I have decided, how-

A

ever, to let the manuscript remain. I will not destroy it, although I will not take the responsibility of printing it. Somebody may think it worth preserving ; and there are two reasons why they may think so, if there are no others. In the first place, it has some little historic value, for I feel increasingly every day that the race to which I belonged is fast passing away, and that the Dissenting minister of the present day is a different being altogether from the Dissenting minister of forty years ago. In the next place, I have observed that the mere knowing that other people have been tried as we have been tried is a consolation to us, and that we are relieved by the assurance that our sufferings are not special and peculiar, but common to us with many others. Death has always been a terror to me, and at times, nay generally, religion and philosophy have been altogether unavailing to mitigate the terror in any way. But it has been a comfort to me to reflect that whatever death may be, it is the inheritance of the whole human race ; that I am not singled out, but shall merely have to pass through what the weakest have had to pass through before me. In the worst of maladies, worst at least to me, those which are hypochondriacal, the healing effect which is produced by the visit of a friend who can simply say "I have endured all that" is most marked. So it is not impossible that some few whose experience has been like mine may, by my example, be freed from that sense of solitude which they find so depressing.

I was born, just before the Liverpool and Manchester Railway was opened, in a small country town in one of the midland shires. It is now semi-manufacturing, at the junction of three or four lines of railway, with hardly a trace left of what it was fifty years ago. It then consisted of one long main street with a few other streets branching from it at right angles. Through this street the mail-coach rattled at night, and the huge waggon rolled through it, drawn by four horses, which twice a week travelled to and from London and brought us what we wanted from the great and unknown city. My father and mother belonged to the ordinary English middle-class of well-to-do shopkeepers. My mother's family came from a little distance, but my father's had lived in those parts for centuries. I remember perfectly well how business used to be carried on in those days. There was absolutely no competition, and although nobody in the town who was in trade got rich, except the banker and the brewer, nearly everybody was tolerably well off, and certainly not pressed with care as their successors are now. The draper, who lived a little way above us, was a deacon in our chapel, and every morning, soon after breakfast, he would start off for his walk of about four miles, stopping by the way to talk to his neighbours about the events of the day. At eleven o'clock, or thereabouts, he would return and would begin work. Everybody used to take an hour for dinner—between one and two, and at that time, especially on a hot July afternoon, the High Street was empty from end to end and the profoundest peace reigned.

My life as a child falls into two portions, sharply divided,—week-day and Sunday. During the week-day I went to the public school, where I learned little or nothing that did me much good. The discipline of the school was admirable, and the head-master was penetrated with a most lofty sense of duty, but the methods of teaching were very imperfect. In Latin we had to learn the Eton Latin Grammar till we knew every word of it by heart, but we did scarcely any retranslation from English into Latin. Much of our time was wasted on the merest trifles, such as learning to write, for example, like copperplate, and, still more extra-ordinary, in copying the letters of the alphabet as they are used in printing. But we had two half-holidays in the week, which seem to me now to have been the happiest part of my life. A river ran through the town, and on summer Wednesdays and Saturdays we wandered along its banks for miles, alternately fishing and bathing. I remember whole afternoons in June, July, and August, passed half naked or altogether naked in the solitary meadows and in the water; I remember the tumbling weir with the deep pool at the bottom into which we dived; I remember, too, the place where we used to swim across the river with our clothes on our heads, because there was no bridge near, and the frequent disaster of a slip of the braces in the middle of the water, so that shirt, jacket, and trousers were soaked, and we had to lie on the grass in the broiling sun without a rag on us till everything was dry again. In winter our joys were of a different kind, but none the less delightful. If it was a frost, we had skating; not like the skating on a London pond, but over long reaches, and if the locks had not intervened, we might have gone a day's journey on the ice without a stoppage. If there was no ice we had football, and what was still better, we could get up a steeple-chase on foot straight across hedge and ditch. In after years, when I lived in London, I came to know children who went to school in Gower Street and travelled backwards and forwards by omnibus, children who had no other recreation than an occasional visit to the Zoological Gardens, or a somewhat sombre walk up to Hampstead to see their aunt; and I have often regretted that they never had any experience of those perfect poetic pleasures which the boy enjoys whose childhood is spent in the country, and whose home is there. A country boarding-school is something altogether different. On the Sundays, however, the compensation came. It was a season of unmixed gloom. My father and mother were rigid Calvinistic Independents, and on that day no newspaper nor any book more secular than the Evangelical Magazine was tolerated. Every preparation for the Sabbath had been made on the Saturday, to avoid as much as possible any work. The meat was cooked beforehand, so that we never had a hot dinner even in the coldest weather; the only thing hot which was permitted was a boiled suet pudding, which cooked itself while we were at chapel, and some potatoes which were prepared after we came home. Not a letter was opened unless it was clearly evident that it was not on business, and for opening these an apology was always offered that it was possible they might contain some announcement of sickness. If on cursory inspection they appeared to be ordinary letters, although they might be from relations or friends, they were put away. After family prayer and breakfast the business of the day began with the Sunday school at nine o'clock. We were taught our Catechism and Bible there till a quarter past ten. We were then marched across the road into the chapel, a large old-fashioned building dating from the time of Charles II. The floor was covered with high pews. The roof was supported by three or four tall wooden pillars which ran from the ground to the ceiling, and the galleries were supported by shorter pillars. There was a large oak pulpit on one side against the wall, and down below, immediately under the minister, was the "singing pew," where the singers and musicians sat, the musicians being performers on the clarionet, flute, violin, and violoncello. Right in front was a long enclosure, called the communion pew, which was usually occupied by a number of the poorer members of the congregation. There were three services every Sunday, besides intermitting prayer-meetings, but these I did not as yet attend. Each service consisted of a hymn, reading the Bible, another hymn, a prayer, the sermon, a third hymn, and a short final prayer. The reading of the Bible was unaccompanied with any observations or explanations, and I do not remember that I ever once heard a mistranslation corrected. The first, or long prayer, as it was called, was a horrible hypocrisy, and it was a sore tax on the preacher to get through it. Anything more totally unlike the model recommended to us in the New Testament cannot well be imagined. It generally began with a confession that we were all sinners, but no individual sins were ever confessed, and then ensued a kind of dialogue with God, very much resembling the speeches which in later years I have heard in the House of Commons from the movers and seconders of addresses to the Crown at the opening of Parliament. In all the religion of that day nothing was falser than the long prayer. Direct appeal to God can only be justified when it is passionate. To come maundering into His presence when we have nothing particular to say is an insult, upon which we should never presume if we had a petition to offer to any earthly personage. We should not venture to take up his time with commonplaces or platitudes; but our minister seemed to consider that the Almighty, who had the universe to govern, had more leisure at His command than the idlest lounger at a club. Nobody ever listened to this performance. I was a good child on the whole, but I am sure I did not, and if the chapel were now in existence, there might be traced on the flap of the pew in which we sat, many curious designs due to these dreary performances. The sermon was not much better. It generally consisted of a text, which

was a mere peg for a discourse, that was pretty much
the same from January to December. The minister
invariably began with the fall of man; propounded
the scheme of redemption, and ended by depicting in
the morning the blessedness of the saints, and in the
evening the doom of the lost. There was a tradition
that in the morning there should be "experience," that
is to say, comfort for the elect, and that the evening
should be appropriated to their less fortunate brethren.
The evening service was the most trying to me of all
these. I never could keep awake, and knew that
to sleep under the Gospel was a sin. The chapel
was lighted in winter by immense chandeliers with
tiers of candles all round. These required perpetual
snuffing, and I can see the old man going round the
chandeliers in the middle of the service with a
mighty pair of snuffers which opened and shut with
a loud click. How I envied him because he had a
semi-secular occupation which prevented that terrible
drowsiness! How I envied the pew-opener, who
was allowed to stand at the vestry door, and could
slip into the vestry every now and then, or even
into the burial-ground if he heard irreverent boys
playing there! The atmosphere of the chapel on
hot nights was most foul, and this added to my dis-
comfort. Oftentimes in winter, when no doors or
windows were open, I have seen the glass panes

streaming with wet inside, and women carried out fainting. On rare occasions I was allowed to go with my father when he went into the villages to preach. As a deacon he was also a lay-preacher, and I had the ride in the gig out and home, and tea at a farmhouse. Perhaps. I shall not have a better opportunity to say that, with all these drawbacks, my religious education did confer upon me some positive advantages. The first was a rigid regard for truthfulness. My parents never would endure a lie or the least equivocation. The second was purity of life, and I look upon this as a simply incalculable gain. Impurity was not an excusable weakness in the society in which I lived; it was a sin for which dreadful punishment was reserved. The reason for my virtue may have been a wrong reason, but anyhow I was saved, and, being saved, much more was saved than health and peace of mind. To this day I do not know where to find a weapon strong enough to subdue the tendency to impurity in young men; and although I cannot tell them what I do not believe, I hanker sometimes after the old prohibitions and penalties. Physio-logical penalties are too remote, and the subtler penalties—the degradation, the growth of callousness to finer pleasures, the loss of sensitiveness to all that is most nobly attractive in woman—are too feeble to withstand temptation when it lies in ambush like a garrotter, and has the reason stunned in a moment. The only thing that can be done is to make the conscience of a boy generally tender, so that he shrinks instinctively from the monstrous injustice of contributing for the sake of his own pleasure to the ruin of another. As soon as manhood dawns, he must also have his attention absorbed on some object which will divert his thoughts intellectually or ideally, and by slight yet constant pressure, exercised not by fits and starts, but day after day, directly and indirectly, his father must form an antipathy in him to brutish selfish sensuality. Above all, there must be no toying with passion, and no books permitted, without condemnation and warning, which are not of a heroic turn. When the boy becomes a man he may read Byron without danger. To a youth he is fatal. Before leaving this subject I may observe, that parents greatly err by not telling their children a good many things which they ought to know. Had I been taught when I was young a few facts about myself, which I only learned accidentally long afterwards, a good deal of misery might have been spared me.

Nothing particular happened to me till I was about fourteen, when I was told it was time I became converted. Conversion, amongst the Independents

and other Puritan sects, is supposed to be a kind of
miracle wrought in the heart by the influence of
the Holy Spirit, by which the man becomes something altogether different to what he was previously.
It affects, or should affect, his character; that is
to say, he ought after conversion to be better in
every way than he was before : but this is not
considered as its main consequence. In its essence
it is a change in the emotions and increased vividness of belief. It is now altogether untrue. Yet it is
an undoubted fact that in earlier days, and, indeed,
in rare cases, as late as the time of my childhood
it was occasionally a reality. It is possible to
imagine that under the preaching of Paul sudden
conviction of a life misspent may have been produced with sudden personal attachment to the
Galilean who, until then, had been despised.
There may have been prompt release of unsuspected
powers, and as prompt an imprisonment for ever
of meaner weaknesses and tendencies; the result
being literally a putting off of the old, and a
putting on of the new man. Love has always been
potent to produce such a transformation, and the exact
counterpart of conversion, as it was understood by
the apostles, may be seen whenever a man is redeemed
from vice by attachment to some woman whom he
worships, or when a girl is reclaimed from idleness

and vanity by becoming a mother. But conversion, as it was understood by me and as it is now understood, is altogether unmeaning. I knew that I had to be "a child of God," and after a time professed myself to be one, but I cannot call to mind that I was anything else than I always had been, save that I was perhaps a little more hypocritical; not in the sense that I professed to others what I knew I did not believe, but in the sense that I professed it to myself. I was obliged to declare myself convinced of sin; convinced of the efficacy of the atonement; convinced that I was forgiven; convinced that the Holy Ghost was shed abroad in my heart; and convinced of a great many other things which were the merest phrases. However, the end of it was that I was proposed for acceptance, and two deacons were deputed, in accordance with the usual custom, to wait upon me and ascertain my fitness for membership. What they said and what I said has now altogether vanished; but I remember with perfect distinctness the day on which I was admitted. It was the custom to demand of each candidate a statement of his or her experience. I had no experience to give; and I was excused on the grounds that I had been the child of pious parents, and consequently had not undergone that convulsion which those, not favoured like myself, necessarily underwent when they were called. I was now expected to attend all those extra services which were specially for the church. I stayed to the late prayer-meeting on Sunday; I went to the prayer-meeting on week-days, and also to private prayer-meetings. These services were not interesting to me for their own sake. I thought they were, but what I really liked was clanship and the satisfaction of belonging to a society marked off from the great world. It must also be added that the evening meetings afforded us many opportunities for walking home with certain young women, who, I am sorry to say, were a more powerful attraction, not to me only but to others, than the prospect of hearing brother Holderness, the travelling draper, confess crimes which, to say the truth, although they were many according to his own account, were never given in that detail which would have made his confession of some value. He never prayed without telling all of us that there was no health in him, and that his soul was a mass of putrifying sores ; but everybody thought the better of him for his self-humiliation. One actual indis-cretion, however, brought home to him would have been visited by suspension or expulsion.

CHAPTER II.

PREPARATION.

IT was necessary that an occupation should be found for me, and after much deliberation it was settled that I should "go into the ministry." I had joined the church, I had "engaged in prayer" publicly, and although I had not set up for being extraordinarily pious, I was thought to be as good as most of the young men who professed to have a mission to regenerate mankind. Accordingly, after some months of preparation, I was taken to a Dissenting College not very far from where we lived. It was a large old-fashioned house with a newer building annexed, and was surrounded with a garden and with meadows. Each student had a separate room, and all had their meat together in a common hall. Altogether there were about forty of us. The establishment consisted of a President, an elderly gentleman who had an American degree of doctor of divinity, and who taught the various branches of theology. He was assisted by three

professors, who imparted to us as much Greek, Latin,
and mathematics as it was considered that we ought
to know. Behold me, then, beginning a course of
training which was to prepare me to meet the doubts
of the nineteenth century; to be the guide of men;
to advise them in their perplexities; to suppress their
tempestuous lusts; to lift them above their petty
cares, and to lead them heavenward! About the
Greek and Latin and the secular part of the college
discipline I will say nothing, except that it was
generally inefficient. The theological and biblical
teaching was a sham. We had come to the college
in the first place to learn the Bible. Our whole
existence was in future to be based upon that book;
our lives were to be passed in preaching it. I will
venture to say that there was no book less understood either by students or professors. The President had a course of lectures, delivered year after
year to successive generations of his pupils, upon its
authenticity and inspiration. They were altogether
remote from the subject, and afterwards, when I
came to know what the difficulties of belief really
were, I found that these essays, which were supposed to be a triumphant confutation of the sceptic,
were a mere sword of lath. They never touched the
question, and if any doubts suggested themselves to
the audience, nobody dared to give them tongue,

lest the expression of them should beget a suspicion of heresy. I remember also some lectures on the proof of the existence of God and on the argument from design; all of which, when my mind was once awakened, were as irrelevant as the chattering of sparrows. When I did not even know who or what this God was, and could not bring my lips to use the word with any mental honesty, of what service was the "watch argument" to me? Very lightly did the President pass over all these initial difficulties of his religion. I see him now, a gentleman with lightish hair, with a most mellifluous voice and a most pastoral manner, reading his prim little tracts to us directed against the "shallow infidel" who seemed to deny conclusions so obvious that we were certain he could not be sincere, and those of us who had never seen an infidel might well be pardoned for supposing that he must always be wickedly blind. About a dozen of these tracts settled the infidel and the whole mass of unbelief from the time of Celsus downwards. The President's task was all the easier because he knew nothing of German literature; and, indeed, the word "German" was a term of reproach signifying something very awful, although nobody knew exactly what it was. Systematic theology was the next science to which the President directed us. We used a sort of Calvinistic manual which began by setting forth that mankind was absolutely in God's power. He was our maker, and we had no legal claim whatever to any consideration from Him. The author then mechanically built up the Calvinistic creed, step by step, like a house of cards. Systematic theology was. the great business of our academical life. We had to read sermons to the President in class, and no sermon was considered complete and proper unless it unfolded what was called the scheme of redemption from beginning to end. So it came to pass that about the Bible, as I have already said, we were in darkness. It was a magazine of texts, and those portions of it, which contributed nothing in the shape of texts or formed no part of the scheme, were neglected. Worse still, not a word was ever spoken to us telling us in what manner to strengthen the reason, to subdue the senses, or in what way to deal with all the varied diseases of that soul of man which we were to set ourselves to save. All its failings, infinitely more complicated than those of the body, were grouped as " sin," and for these there was one quack remedy. If the patient did not like the remedy, or got no good from it, the fault was his. It is remarkable that the scheme was never of the slightest service to me in repressing one solitary evil inclination; at no point did it come into contact with me. At the time it seemed right and proper that I should learn it, and I had no doubt of its efficacy; but when the stress of temptation was upon me, it never occurred to me, nor when I became a minister did I find it sufficiently powerful to mend the most trifling fault. In after years, but not till I had strayed far away from the President and his creed, the Bible was really opened to me, and became to me, what it now is, the most precious of books.

There were several small chapels scattered in the villages near the college, and these chapels were "supplied," as the phrase is, by the students. Those who were near the end of their course were also employed as substitutes for regular ministers when they were temporarily absent. Sometimes a senior was even sent up to London to take the place, on a sudden emergency, of a great London minister, and when he came back he was an object almost of adoration. The congregation, on the other hand, consisting in some part of country people spending a Sunday in town and anxious to hear a celebrated preacher, were not at all disposed to adore, when, instead of the great man, they saw "only a student." By the time I was nineteen I took my turn in "supplying" the villages, and set forth with the utmost confidence what appeared to me to be the indubitable gospel. No shadow of a suspicion of its

truth ever crossed my mind, and yet I had not spent
an hour in comprehending, much less in answering,
one objection to it.   The objections, in fact, had
never met me; they were over my horizon altogether.   It is wonderful to think how I could take
so much for granted; and not merely take it to
myself and for myself, but proclaim it as a message
to other people.   It would be a mistake, however,
to suppose that theological youths are the only class
who are guilty of such presumption.   Our gregarious
instinct is so strong that it is the most difficult
thing for us to be satisfied with suspended judgment.
Men must join a party and have a cry, and they
generally take up their party and their cry from the
most indifferent motives.   For my own part I cannot
be enthusiastic about politics, except on rare occasions when the issue is a very narrow one.   There is
so much that requires profound examination, and it
disgusts me to get upon a platform and dispute with
ardent Radicals or Conservatives who know nothing
about even the rudiments of history, political economy,
or political philosophy, without which it is as absurd
to have an opinion upon what are called politics as
it would be to have an opinion upon an astronomical
problem without having learned Euclid.   The more
incapable we are of thorough investigation, the wider
and deeper are the subjects upon which we busy

ourselves, and still more strange, the more bigoted
do we become in our conclusions about them; and
yet it is not strange, for he who by painful processes
has found yes and no alternate for so long that he
is not sure which is final, is the last man in the
world, if he for the present is resting in yes, to
crucify another who can get no further than no.
The bigot is he to whom no such painful processes
have ever been permitted.

The society amongst the students was very poor.
Not a single friendship formed then has remained
with me. They were mostly young men of no
education, who had been taken from the counter,
and their spiritual life was not very deep. In many
of them it did not even exist, and their whole
attention was absorbed upon their chances of
getting wealthy congregations or of making desirable
matches. It was a time in which the world outside
was seething with the ferment which had been cast
into it by Germany and by those in England whom
Germany had influenced, but not a fragment of it
had dropped within our walls. I cannot call to
mind a single conversation upon any but the most
trivial topics, nor did our talk ever turn even upon
our religion, so far as it was a thing affecting the
soul, but only upon it as something subsidiary to
chapels, "causes," deacons, and the like. The

emptiness of some of my colleagues and their world-liness too were almost incredible. There was one who was particularly silly. He was a blonde youth with greyish eyes, a mouth not quite shut, and an eternal simper upon his face. He never had an idea in his head, and never read anything except the denominational newspapers and a few well-known aids to sermonising. He was a great man at all tea-meetings, anniversaries, and parties. He was facile in public speaking, and he dwelt much upon the joys of heaven and upon such topics as the possibility of our recognising one another there. I have known him describe for twenty minutes, in a kind of watery rhetoric, the passage of the soul to bliss through death and its meeting in the next world with those who had gone before. With all his weakness he was close and mean in money matters, and when he left college, the first thing he did was to marry a widow with a fortune. Before long he became one of the most popular of ministers in a town much visited by sick persons, with whom he was an especial favourite. I disliked him—and specially disliked his unpleasant behaviour to women. If I had been a woman I should have spurned him for his perpetual insult of inane compliments. He was always dawdling after " the sex," which was one of his sweet phrases, and yet he was not passionate.

Passion does not dawdle and compliment, nor is it nasty, as this fellow was. Passion may burn like a devouring flame; and in a few moments, like flame, may bring down a temple to dust and ashes, but it is earnest as flame, and essentially pure.

During the first two years at college my life was entirely external. My heart was altogether untouched by anything I heard, read, or did, although I myself supposed that I took an interest in them. But one day in my third year, a day I remember as well as Paul must have remembered afterwards the day on which he went to Damascus, I happened to find amongst a parcel of books a volume of poems in paper boards. It was called "Lyrical Ballads," and I read first one and then the whole book. It conveyed to me no new doctrine, and yet the change it wrought in me could only be compared with that which is said to have been wrought on Paul himself by the Divine apparition. Looking over the "Lyrical Ballads" again, as I have looked over it a dozen times since then, I can hardly see what it was which stirred me so powerfully, nor do I believe that it communicated much to me which could be put in words. But it excited a movement and a growth which went on till, by degrees, all the systems which enveloped me like a body gradually decayed from me and fell away into nothing. Of more importance

too than the decay of systems was the birth of a
habit of inner reference and a dislike to occupy
myself with anything which did not in some way
or other touch the soul, or was not the illustration
or embodiment of some spiritual law. There is, of
course, a definite explanation to be given of one
effect produced by the "Lyrical Ballads." God is
nowhere formally deposed, and Wordsworth would
have been the last man to say that he had lost his
faith in the God of his fathers. But his real God is
not the God of the Church but the God of the hills,
the abstraction Nature, and to this my reverence was
transferred. Instead of an object of worship which
was altogether artificial, remote, never coming into
genuine contact with me, I had now one which I
thought to be real, one in which literally I could
live and move and have my being, an actual fact
present before my eyes. God was brought from
that heaven of the books, and resided on the downs
visible in the far-away distances seen from the top
of a hill and in every cloud-shadow which wandered
across the valley. Wordsworth unconsciously did for
me what every religious reformer has done,—he
recreated my Supreme Divinity, substituting a new
and living spirit for the old deity, once alive but
gradually hardened into an idol.

What days were those of the next few years before

increasing age had presented preciser problems and
demanded preciser answers; before all joy was
darkened by the shadow of on-coming death, and
when life seemed infinite! Those were the days when
through the whole long summer's morning I wanted
no companion but myself, provided only I was in
the country, and when books were read with tears
in the eyes. Those were the days when mere life,
apart from anything which it brings, was exquisite.
In my own college I found no sympathy, but we
were in the habit of meeting occasionally the students
from other colleges, and amongst them I met with
one or two, especially one who had undergone
experiences similar to my own. The friendships
formed with these young men have lasted till now,
and have been the most permanent of all the
relationships of my existence. I wish not to judge
others, but the persons who to me have proved themselves most attractive, have been those who have
passed through such a process as that through which
I myself passed; those who have had in some form
or other an enthusiastic stage in their history, when
the story of Genesis and of the Gospels has been
rewritten, when God has visibly walked in the
garden, and the Son of God has drawn men away
from their daily occupations into the divinest of
dreams. I have known men—most interesting men—

with far greater powers than any which I have possessed, men who have never been trammelled by a false creed, who have devoted themselves to science and acquired a great reputation, who have somehow never laid hold upon me like the man I have just mentioned. He failed altogether as a minister and went back to his shop, but the old glow of his youth burns, and will burn for ever. When I am with him our conversation naturally turns on matters which are of profoundest importance : with others it may be instructive, but I leave them unmoved, and I trace the difference distinctly to that visitation, for it was nothing else, which came to him in his youth.

The effect which was produced upon my preaching and daily conversation by this change was immediate. It became gradually impossible for me to talk about subjects which had not some genuine connection with me, or to desire to hear others talk about them. The artificial, the merely miraculous, the event which had no inner meaning, no matter how large externally it might be, I did not care for. A little Greek mythological story would be of more importance to me than a war which filled the newspapers. What then could I do with my theological treatises. It would be a mistake, however, to suppose that I immediately became formally heretical. Nearly every doctrine

in the college creed had once had a natural origin
in the necessities of human nature, and might therefore be so interpreted as to become a necessity
again. To reach through to that original necessity;
to explain the atonement as I believed it appeared
to Paul, and the sinfulness of man as it appeared
to the prophets, was my object. But it was precisely this reaching after a meaning which consti-
tuted heresy. The distinctive essence of our orthodoxy was not this or that dogma, but the acceptance
of dogmas as communications from without, and
not as born from within. Heresy began, and in
fact was altogether present, when I said to myself
that a mere statement of the atonement as taught
in class was impossible for me, and that I must go
back to Paul and his century, place myself in his
position, and connect the atonement through him with
something which I felt. I thus continued to use all
the terms which I had hitherto used; but an uneasy
feeling began to develop itself about me in the
minds of the professors, because I did not rest in
the "simplicity" of the gospel. To me this meant
its unintelligibility. I remember, for example, discoursing about the death of Christ. There was not
a single word which was ordinarily used in the
pulpit, which I did not use,—satisfaction for sin,
penalty, redeeming blood, they were all there,—but

I began by saying that in this world there was no redemption for man but by blood; furthermore, the innocent had everywhere and in all time to suffer for the guilty. It had been objected that it was contrary to our notion of an all-loving Being that He should demand such a sacrifice; but, contrary or not, in this world it was true, quite apart from Jesus, that virtue was martyred every day, unknown and unconsoled, in order that the wicked might somehow be saved. This was part of the scheme of the world, and we might dislike it or not, we could not get rid of it. The consequences of my sin, moreover, are rendered less terrible by virtues not my own. I am literally saved from penalties because another pays the penalty for me. The atonement, and what it accomplished for man, were therefore a sublime summing up as it were of what sublime men have to do for their race; an exemplification, rather than a contradiction, of Nature herself, as we know her in our own experience. Now, all this was really intended as a defence of the atonement; but the President heard me that Sunday, and on the Monday he called me into his room. He said that my sermon was marked by considerable ability, but he should have been better satisfied if I had confined myself to setting forth as plainly as I could the "way of salvation" as revealed in Christ Jesus. What I had urged might perhaps have possessed some interest for cultivated people; in fact, he had himself urged pretty much the same thing many years ago, when he was a young man, in a sermon he had preached at the Union meeting, but I must recollect that in all probability my sphere of usefulness would lie amongst humble hearers, perhaps in an agricultural village or a small town, and that he did not think people of this sort would understand me if I talked over their heads as I had done the day before. What they wanted on a Sunday, after all the cares of the week, was not anything to perplex and disturb them; not anything which demanded any exercise of thought; but a repetition of the "old story of which, Mr. Rutherford, you know we never ought to get weary; an exhibition of our exceeding sinfulness; of our safety in the Rock of Ages, and there only; of the joys of the saints and the sufferings of those who do not believe." His words fell on me like the hand of a corpse, and I went away much depressed. My sermon had excited me, and the man who of all men ought to have welcomed me, had not a word of warmth or encouragement for me, nothing but the coldest indifference, and even repulse.

It occurs to me here to offer an explanation of a failing of which I have been accused in later years, and that is secrecy and reserve. The real truth is, that nobody more than myself could desire self-revelation; but owing to peculiar tendencies in me, and peculiarity of education, I was always prone to say things in conversation which I found produced blank silence in the majority of those who listened to me, and immediate opportunity was taken by my hearers to turn to something trivial. Hence it came to pass that only when tempted by unmistakable sympathy could I be induced to express my real self on any topic of importance. It is a curious instance of the difficulty of diagnosing (to use a doctor's word) any spiritual disease, if disease this shyness may be called. People would ordinarily set it down to self-reliance, with no healthy need of intercourse. It was nothing of the kind. It was an excess of communicativeness, an eagerness to show what was most at my heart, and to ascertain what was at the heart of those to whom I talked, which made me incapable of mere fencing and trifling, and so often caused me to retreat into myself when I found absolute absence of response.

I am also reminded here of a dream which I had in these years of a perfect friendship. I always felt that talk with whom I would I left something unsaid which was precisely what I most wished to say. I wanted a friend who would sacrifice himself to me

utterly, and to whom I might offer a similar sacrifice.
I found companions for whom I cared, and who professed to care for me ; but I was thirsting for deeper
draughts of love than any which they had to offer ;
and I said to myself that if I were to die, not one
of them would remember me for more than a week.
This was not selfishness, for I longed to prove my
devotion as well as to receive that of another. How
this ideal haunted me! It made me restless and
anxious at the sight of every new face, wondering
whether at last I had found that for which I
searched as if for the kingdom of heaven. It is
superfluous to say that a friend of the kind I wanted
never appeared, and disappointment after disappointment at last produced in me a cynicism which
repelled people from me, and brought upon me a
good deal of suffering. I tried men by my standard,
and if they did not come up to it I rejected them ;
thus I prodigally wasted a good deal of the affection
which the world would have given me. Only when
I got much older did I discern the duty of accepting
life as God has made it, and thankfully receiving any
scrap of love offered to me, however imperfect it
might be. I don't know any mistake which I have
made which has cost me more than this; but at the
same time I must record that it was a mistake for
which, considering everything, I cannot much blame

myself. I hope it is amended now. Now when it is getting late I recognise a higher obligation, brought home to me by a closer study of the New Testament. Sympathy or no sympathy, a man's love should no more fail towards his fellows than that love which spent itself on disciples who altogether misunderstood it, like the rain which falls on just and unjust alike.

CHAPTER III.

WATER LANE.

I HAD now reached the end of my fourth year at college, and it was time for me to leave. I was sent down into the eastern counties to a congregation which had lost its minister, and was there " on probation" for a month. I was naturally a good speaker, and as the " cause" had got very low, the attendance at the chapel increased during the month I was there. The deacons thought they had a prospect of returning prosperity, and in the end I received a nearly unanimous invitation, which after some hesitation I accepted. One of the deacons, a Mr. Snale, was against me ; he thought I was not " quite sound," but he was overruled. We shall hear more of him presently. After a short holiday I entered on my new duties. The town was one of those which are not uncommon in that part of the world. It had a population of about seven or eight thousand, and

C

was a sort of condensation of the agricultural country
round. There was one main street, consisting prin-
cipally of very decent, respectable shops. Generally
speaking, there were two shops of each trade; one
which was patronized by the Church and Tories, and
another by the Dissenters and Whigs. The inhabi-
tants were divided into two distinct camps—of the
Church and Tory camp the other camp knew nothing.
On the other hand, the knowledge which each member
of the Dissenting camp had of every other member was
most intimate. The Dissenters were further split up
into two or three different sects, but the main sect
was that of the Independents. They, in fact, domi-
nated every other. There was a small Baptist com-
munity, and the Wesleyans had a new red brick chapel
in the outskirts; but for some reason or other the Independents were really the Dissenters, and until the
" cause " had dwindled, as before observed, all the Dissenters of any note were to be found on Sunday in their
meeting-house in Water Lane. My predecessor had
died in harness at the age of seventy-five. I never
knew him, but from all I could hear he must have been
a man of some power. As he got older, however, he
became feeble; and after a course of three sermons
on a Sunday for fifty years, what he had to say was
so entirely anticipated by his congregation, that
although they all maintained that the gospel, or

in other words, the doctrine of the fall, the atonement, and so forth, should continually be presented, and their minister also believed and acted implicitly upon the same theory, they fell away,—some to the Baptists, some to the neighbouring Independents about two miles off, and some to the Church, while a few "went nowhere." When I came I found that the deacons still remained true. They were the skeleton; but the flesh was so wofully emaciated, that on my first Sunday there were not above fifty persons in a building which would hold seven hundred. These deacons were four in number. One was an old farmer who lived in a village three miles distant. Ever since he was a boy he had driven over to Water Lane on Sunday. He and his family brought their dinner with them and ate it in the vestry; but they never stopped till the evening, because of the difficulty of getting home on dark nights, and because they all went to bed in winter time at eight o'clock. Morning and afternoon Mr. Catfield—for that was his name—gave out the hymns. He was a plain, honest man, very kind, very ignorant, never reading any book except the Bible, and barely a newspaper save *Bell's Weekly Messenger*. Even about the Bible he knew little or nothing beyond a few favourite chapters; and I am bound to say that, so far as my experience goes, the character so frequently drawn in romances of intense Bible students in Dissenting congregations is very rare. At the same time Mr. Catfield believed himself to be very orthodox, and in his way was very pious. I could never call him a hypocrite. He was as sincere as he could be, and yet no religious expression of his was ever so sincere as the most ordinary expression of the most trifling pleasure or pain. The second deacon, Mr. Weeley, was, as he described himself, a builder and undertaker; more properly an undertaker and carpenter. He was a thin, tall man, with a tenor voice, and he set the tunes. He was entirely without energy of any kind, and always seemed oppressed by a world which was too much for him. He had depended a good deal for custom upon his chapel connection; and when the attendance at the chapel fell off, his trade fell off likewise, so that he had to compound with his creditors. He was a mere shadow, a man of whom nothing could be said either good or evil. The third deacon was Mr. Snale, the draper. When I first knew him he was about thirty-five. He was slim, small, and small-faced; closely shaven excepting a pair of little curly whiskers, and he was extremely neat. He had a little voice too, rather squeaky, and the marked peculiarity that he hardly ever said anything, no matter how disagreeable it might be, without stretching as if in a smile his thin little lips. He kept the principal draper's shop in the town, and even Church people spent their money with him, because he was so very genteel compared with the other draper, who was a great red man, and hung things outside his window. Mr. Snale was married, had children, and was strictly proper. But his way of talking to women and about them was more odious than the way of a debauchee. He invariably called them "the ladies," or more exactly, "the leedies;" and he hardly ever spoke to a "leedy" without a smirk and some faint attempt at a joke. One of the customs of the chapel was what were called Dorcas meetings. Once a month the wives and daughters drank tea with each other; the evening being ostensibly devoted to making clothes for the poor. The husband of the lady who gave the entertainment for the month had to wait upon the company, and the minister was expected to read to them while they worked. It was my lot to be Mr. Snale's guest two or three times when Mrs. Snale was the Dorcas hostess. We used all of us to assemble in the drawing-room, which was over the shop and looked out into the town market-place. There was a round table in the middle of the room, at which Mrs. Snale sat and made the tea. Abundance of hot buttered toast and muffins were provided, which Mr. Snale and a maid handed round to the party. Four pictures decorated the walls. One hung over the mantelpiece. It was a portrait in oils of Mr. Snale, and opposite to it, on the other side, was a portrait of Mrs. Snale. Both were daubs, but curiously faithful in depicting what was most offensive in the character of both the originals, Mr. Snale's simper being preserved; together with the peculiar hard, heavy sensuality of the eye in Mrs. Snale, who was large and full-faced, correct like Mr. Snale, and a member of the church, but a woman whom I never saw moved to any generosity; and cruel, not with the ferocity of the tiger, but with the dull insensibility of a cart wheel which will roll over a man's neck as easily as over a flint. The third picture represented the descent of the Holy Ghost: a number of persons sitting in a chamber, and each one with the flame of a candle on his head. The fourth represented the last day. The Son of God was in a chair surrounded by clouds, and beside Him was a flying figure blowing a long mail-coach horn. The dead were coming up out of their graves; some were half out of the earth, others three parts out—the whole of the bottom part of the picture being filled with bodies emerging from the ground, a few looking happy, but most of them very wretched; all of them being naked. The first time I went to Mrs. Snale's Dorcas gathering Mr. Snale was reader, as I was a novice; and I was

very glad to resign the task to him. As the business
in hand was week-day and secular, it was not considered necessary that the selected subjects should
be religious; but as it was distinctly connected with
the chapel, it was also considered that they should
have a religious flavour. Consequently the Bible
was excluded, and so were books on topics altogether
worldly. Dorcas meetings were generally, therefore,
shut up to the denominational journal and to
magazines. Towards the end of the evening Mr.
Snale read the births, deaths, and marriages in this
journal. It would not have been thought right to
read them·from any other newspaper, but it was
agreed, with a fineness of tact which was very
remarkable, that it was quite right to read them in
one which was "serious." During the whole time
that the reading was going on conversation was not
arrested, but was conducted in a kind of half whisper;
and this was another reason why I exceedingly disliked to read, as I could never endure to speak, if
people did not listen. At half-past eight the work
was put away, and Mrs. Snale went to the piano
and played a hymn tune, the minister having first
of all selected the hymn. Singing over, he offered
a short prayer, and the company separated. Supper
was not served, as it was found to be too great an
expense. The husbands of the ladies generally

came to escort them home, but did not come up-stairs. Some of the gentlemen waited below in the dining-room, but most of them preferred the shop, for although it was shut, the gas was burning to enable the assistants to put away the goods which had been got out during the day. When it first became my turn to read I proposed the " Vicar of Wakefield ; " but although no objection was raised at the time, Mr. Snale took an opportunity of telling me, after I had got through a chapter or two, that he thought it would be better if it were discontinued. " Because you know, Mr. Rutherford," he said, with his smirk, " the company is mixed; there are young leedies present, and *perhaps*, Mr. Rutherford, a book with a more requisite tone might be more suitable on such an occasion." What he meant I did not know, and how to find a book with a more requisite tone I did not know. However the next time, in my folly, I tried a selection from George Fox's Journal. Mr. Snale objected to this too. It was " hardly of a character adapted for social intercourse," he thought ; and furthermore " although Mr. Fox might be a very good man, and was a converted character, yet he did not, you know, Mr. Rutherford, belong to us." So I was reduced to that class of literature which of all others I most abominated and which always seemed to me the most profane,—religious and sectarian gossip, religious novels designed to make religion attractive, and other slip-slop of this kind. I could not endure it, and was frequently unwell on Dorcas evenings.

The rest of the small congregation was of no particular note. As I have said before it had greatly fallen away, and all who remained clung to the chapel rather by force of habit than from any other reason. The only exception was an old maiden lady and her sister, who lived in a little cottage about a mile out of the town. They were pious in the purest sense of the word, suffering much from ill-health, but perfectly resigned, and with a kind of tempered cheerfulness always apparent on their faces, like the cheerfulness of a white sky with a sun veiled by light and lofty clouds. They were the daughters of a gentleman farmer who had left them a small annuity. Their house was one of the sweetest which I ever entered. The moment I found myself inside it, I became conscious of perfect repose. Everything was at rest, books, pictures, furniture, all breathed the same peace. Nothing in the house was new, but everything had been preserved with such care that nothing looked old. Yet the owners were not what is called old-maidish ; that is to say, they were not superstitious worshippers of order and neatness. I remember Mrs. Snale's children coming in one afternoon when I was there. They were rough and ill-mannered, and left traces of dirty footmarks all over the carpet, which the two ladies noticed at once. But it made no difference to the treatment of the children, who had some cake and currant wine given to them, and were sent away rejoicing. Directly they had gone, the eldest of my friends asked me if I would excuse her; she would gather up the dirt before it was trodden about. So she brought a dust-pan and brush (the little servant was out) and patiently swept the floor. That was the way with them. Did any mischief befall them or those whom they knew; without blaming anybody, they immediately and noiselessly set about repairing it with that silent promptitude of nature which rebels not against a wound, but the very next instant begins her work of protection and recovery. The Misses Arbour (for that was their name) mixed but little in the society of the town. They explained to me that their health would not permit it. They read books— a few—but they were not books about which I knew very much, and they belonged altogether to an age preceding mine. Of the names which had moved me and of all the thoughts stirring in the time, they had heard nothing. They greatly admired Cowper, a poet who then did not much attract me.

The country near me was rather level, but towards

the west it rose into soft swelling hills between which were pleasant lanes. At about ten miles distant eastward was the sea. A small river ran across the High Street under a stone bridge; for about two miles below us it was locked up for the sake of the mills, but at the end of the two miles it became tidal and flowed between deep and muddy banks through marshes to the ocean. Almost all my walks were by the river bank down to these marshes, and as far on as possible till the open water was visible. Not that I did not like inland scenery : nobody could like it more, but the sea was a corrective to the littleness all round me. With the ships on it sailing to the other end of the earth it seemed to connect me with the great world outside the parochialism of the society in which I lived.

Such was the town of C——, and such the company amidst which I found myself. After my probation it was arranged that I should begin my new duties at once, and accordingly I took lodgings, —two rooms over the shop of a tailor who acted as chapel-keeper, pew-opener, and sexton. There was a small endowment on the chapel of fifty pounds a year, and the rest of my income was derived from the pew-rents, which at the time I took charge did not exceed another seventy. The first Sunday on which I preached after being accepted was a dull day in November, but there was no dulness in me. The congregation had increased a good deal during the past four weeks, and I was stimulated by the prospect of the new life before me. It seemed to be a fit opportunity to say something generally about Christianity and its special peculiarities. I began by pointing out that each philosophy and religion which had arisen in the world was the answer to a question earnestly asked at the time; it was a remedy proposed to meet some extreme pressure. Religions and philosophies were not created by idle people who sat down and said, " Let us build up a system of beliefs upon the universe ; what shall we say about immortality, about sin," and so on. Unless there had been antecedent necessity there could be no religion ; and no problem of life or death could be solved except under the weight of that necessity. The stoical morality arose out of the condition of Rome when the scholar and the pious man could do nothing but simply strengthen his knees and back to bear an inevitable burden. He was forced to find some counterpoise for the misery of poverty and persecution, and he found it in the denial of their power to touch him. So with Christianity. Jesus was a poor solitary thinker, confronted by two enormous and overpowering organisations, the Jewish hierarchy and the Roman state. He taught the doctrine of the kingdom of heaven; He trained Himself to have faith in the absolute monarchy of the soul, the absolute monarchy of His own; He tells us that each man should learn to find peace in his own thoughts, his own visions. It is a most difficult thing to do; most difficult to believe that my highest happiness consists in *my* perception of whatever is beautiful. If I by myself watch the sun rise, or the stars come out in the evening, or feel the love of man or woman, I ought to say to myself, " There is nothing beyond this." But people will not rest there; they are not content, and they are for ever chasing a shadow which flies before them, a something external which never brings what it promises. I said that Christianity was essentially the religion of the unknown and of the lonely; of those who were not a success. It was the religion of the man who went through life thinking much, but who made few friends and saw nothing come of his thoughts. I said a good deal more upon the same theme which I have forgotten. After the service was over I went down into the vestry. Nobody came near me but my landlord, the chapel keeper, who said it was raining, and immediately went away to put out the lights and shut up the building. I had no umbrella, and there was nothing to be done but to walk out in the wet. When I

got home I found that my supper, consisting of
bread and cheese with a pint of beer, was on the
table, but apparently it had been thought unnecessary to light the fire again at that time of night.
I was overwrought, and paced about for hours in
hysterics. All that I had been preaching seemed
the merest vanity when I was brought face to face
with the fact itself; and I reproached myself bitterly
that my own creed would not stand the stress of an
hour's actual trial. Towards morning I got into bed,
but not to sleep, and when the dull daylight of
Monday came, all support had vanished, and I
seemed to be sinking into a bottomless abyss. I
became gradually worse week by week, and my
melancholy took a fixed form. I got a notion into
my head that my brain was failing, and this was
my first acquaintance with that most awful malady
hypochondria. I did not know then what I know
now, although I only half believe it practically, that
this fixity of form is a frequent symptom of the disease, and that the general weakness manifests itself
in a determinate horror, which gradually fades with
returning health. For months—many months, this
dreadful conviction of coming idiotcy or insanity lay
upon me like some poisonous reptile with its fangs
driven into my very marrow, so that I could not
shake it off. It went with me wherever I went, it got

up with me in the morning, walked about with me
all day, and lay down with me at night. I managed
somehow or other to do my work, but I prayed incessantly for death; and to such a state was I reduced
that I could not even make the commonest appointment for a day beforehand. The mere knowledge that
something had to be done agitated me and prevented
my doing it. In June, next year, my holiday came,
and I went away home to my father's house. Father
and mother were going for the first time in their
lives to spend a few days by the seaside together, and
I went with them to Ilfracombe. I had been there
about a week, when on one memorable morning, on
the top of one of those Devonshire hills, I became
aware of a kind of flush in the brain and a momen-
tary relief such as I had not known since that
November night. I seemed, far away on the horizon,
to see just a rim of olive light low down under the
edge of the leaden cloud that hung over my head, a
prophecy of the restoration of the sun, or at least a
witness that somewhere it shone. It was not permanent, and perhaps the gloom was never more
profound, nor the agony more intense, than it was
for long after my Ilfracombe visit. But the light
broadened, and gradually the darkness was miti-
gated. I have never been thoroughly restored.
Often, with no warning, I am plunged in the Valley

of the Shadow, and no outlet seems possible; but I contrive to traverse it, or to wait in calmness for access of strength. When I was at my worst I went to see a doctor. He recommended me stimulants. I had always been rather abstemious, and he thought I was suffering from physical weakness. At first wine gave me relief, and such marked relief that whenever I felt my misery insupportable I turned to the bottle. At no time in my life was I ever the worse for liquor, but I soon found the craving for it was getting the better of me. I resolved never to touch it except at night, and kept my vow; but the consequence was that I looked forward to the night, and waited for it with such eagerness that the day seemed to exist only for the sake of the evening, when I might hope at least for rest. For the wine as wine I cared nothing; anything that would have dulled my senses would have done just as well. But now a new terror developed itself. I began to be afraid that I was becoming a slave to alcohol; that the passion for it would grow upon me, and that I should disgrace myself, and die the most contemptible of all deaths. To a certain extent my fears were just. The dose which was necessary to procure temporary forgetfulness of my trouble had to be increased, and might have increased dangerously. But one day feeling more than usual the tyranny of

my master, I received strength to make a sudden
resolution to cast him off utterly. Whatever be the
consequence, I said, I will not be the victim of this
shame. If I am to go down to the grave, it shall
be as a man, and I will bear what I have to bear
honestly and without resort to the base evasion of
stupefaction. So that night I went to bed having
drunk nothing but water. The struggle was not
felt just then. It came later, when the first enthusiasm of a new purpose had faded away, and I had
to fall back on mere force of will. I don't think
anybody but those who have gone through such a
crisis can comprehend what it is. I never understood the maniacal craving which is begotten by
ardent spirits, but I understood enough to be convinced that the man who has once rescued himself
from the domination even of half a bottle, or three-
parts of a bottle of claret daily, may assure himself
that there is nothing more in life to be done which
he need dread. Two or three remarks begotten of
experience in this matter deserve record. One is
that the most powerful inducement to abstinence, in
my case, was the interference of wine with liberty,
and above all things its interference with what I
really loved best, and the transference of desire from
what was most desirable to what was sensual and
base. The morning, instead of being spent in quiet

D

contemplation and quiet pleasures, was spent in degrading anticipations. What enabled me to conquer, was not so much heroism as a susceptibility to nobler joys, and the difficulty which a man must encounter who is not susceptible to them must be enormous and almost insuperable. Pity, profound pity is his due, and especially if he happen to possess a nervous, emotional organisation. If we want to make men water-drinkers, we must first of all awaken in them a capacity for being tempted by delights which water-drinking intensifies. The mere preaching of self-denial will do little or no good. Another observation is, that there is no danger in stopping at once, and suddenly, the habit of drinking. The prisons and asylums furnish ample evidence upon that point, but there will be many an hour of exhaustion in which this danger will be simulated and wine will appear the proper remedy. No man, or at least very few men, would ever feel any desire for it soon after sleep. This shows the power of repose, and I would advise anybody who may be in earnest in this matter to be specially on guard during moments of physical fatigue, and to try the effect of eating and rest. Do not persist in a blind, obstinate wrestle. Simply take food, drink water, go to bed, and so conquer not by brute strength, but by strategy. Going back to hypochondria and its countless forms

of agony, let it be borne in mind that the first thing
to be aimed at is patience—not to get excited with
fears, not to dread the evil which most probably
will never arrive, but to sit down quietly and *wait*.
The simpler and less stimulating the diet, the more
likely it is that the sufferer will be able to watch
through the wakeful hours without delirium, and the
less likely is it that the general health will be im-
paired. Upon this point of health too much stress cannot be laid. It is difficult for the victim to believe that
his digestion has anything to do with a disease which
seems so purely spiritual, but frequently the misery
will break up and yield, if it do not altogether dis-
appear, by a little attention to physiology and by a
change of air. As time wears on, too, mere duration
will be a relief; for it familiarises with what at first
was strange and insupportable, it shows the ground-
lessness of fears, and it enables us to say with each
new paroxysm, that we have surmounted one like it
before, and probably a worse.

CHAPTER IV.

EDWARD GIBBON MARDON.

I HAD now been "settled," to use a dissenting phrase, for nearly eighteen months. While I was ill I had no heart in my work, and the sermons I preached were very poor and excited no particular suspicion. But with gradually returning energy my love of reading revived, and questions which had slumbered again presented themselves. I continued for some time to deal with them as I had dealt with the atonement at college. I said that Jesus was the true Paschal Lamb, for that by His death men were saved from their sins, and from the consequences of them; I said that belief in Christ, that is to say, a love for Him, was more powerful to redeem men than the works of the law. All this may have been true, but truth lies in relation. It was not true when I, understanding what I understood by it, taught it to men who professed to believe in the Westminster confession. The preacher who preaches

it uses a vocabulary which has a certain definite
meaning, and has had this meaning for centuries.
He cannot stay to put his own interpretation upon
it whenever it is upon his lips, and so his hearers
are in a false position and imagine him to be much
more orthodox than he really is. For some time I
fell into this snare, until one day I happened to be
reading the story of Balaam. Balaam, though most
desirous to prophesy smooth things for Balak, had
nevertheless a word put into his mouth by God.
When he came to Balak he was unable to curse,
and could do nothing but bless. Balak, much dis-
satisfied, thought that a change of position might
alter Balaam's temper, and he brought him away
from the high places of Baal to the field of Zophim,
to the top of Pisgah. But Balaam could do nothing
better even on Pisgah. Not even a compromise
was possible, and the second blessing was more
emphatic than the first. "God," cried the prophet,
pressed sorely by his message, "is not a man, that He
should lie; neither the son of man, that He should
repent: hath He said, and shall He not do it? or
hath He spoken, and shall He not make it good?
Behold, I have received commandment to bless:
and He hath blessed; and I cannot reverse it." This
was very unsatisfactory, and Balaam was asked, if
he could not curse, at least to refrain from benedic-

tion. The answer was still the same. "Told not I
thee, saying, All that the Lord speaketh, that I must
do?" A third shift was tried, and Balaam went to
the top of Peor. This was worse than ever. The
spirit of the Lord came upon him, and he broke out
into triumphal anticipation of the future glories of
Israel. Balak remonstrated in wrath, but Balaam
was altogether inaccessible. "If Balak would give
me his house full of silver and gold, I cannot go
beyond the commandment of the Lord, to do either
good or bad of mine own mind; but what the Lord
saith, that will I speak." This story greatly impressed me, and I date from it a distinct disinclina-
tion to tamper with myself, or to deliver what I had
to deliver in phrases which, though they might be
conciliatory, were misleading.

About this time there was a movement in the
town to obtain a better supply of water. The soil
was gravelly and full of cesspools, side by side with
which were sunk the wells. A public meeting was
held, and I attended and spoke on behalf of the
scheme. There was much opposition, mainly on the
score that the rates would be increased, and on the
Saturday after the meeting the following letter
appeared in the *Sentinel*, the local paper:—

"SIR,—It is not my desire to enter into the con- ·

troversy now raging about the water supply of this town, but I must say I was much surprised that a minister of religion should interfere in politics. Sir, I cannot help thinking that if the said minister would devote himself to the Water of Life,—

> 'that gentle fount
> Progressing from Immanuel's mount,'—

it would be much more harmonious with his function as a follower of him who knew nothing save Christ crucified. Sir, I have no wish to introduce controversial topics upon a subject like religion into your columns, which are allotted to a different line, but I must be permitted to observe that I fail to see how a minister's usefulness can be stimulated if he sets class against class. Like the widows in affliction of old, he should keep himself pure and unspotted from the world. How can many of us accept the glorious gospel on the Sabbath from a man who will incur spots during the week by arguing about cesspools like any other man? Sir, I will say nothing, moreover, about a minister of the gospel assisting to bind burdens—that is to say, rates and taxation—upon the shoulders of men, grievous to be borne. Surely, sir, a minister of the Lamb of God, who was shed for the remission of sins, should be *against* burdens.—I am, sir, your obedient servant, A CHRISTIAN TRADESMAN."

I had not the least doubt as to the authorship of this precious epistle. Mr. Snale's hand was apparent in every word. He was fond of making religious verses, and once we were compelled to hear the Sunday-school children sing a hymn which he had composed. The two lines of poetry were undoubtedly his. Furthermore, although he had been a chapel-goer all his life, he muddled, invariably, passages from the Bible. They had no definite meaning for him, and there was nothing consequently to prevent his tacking the end of one verse to the beginning of another. Mr. Snale, too, continually "failed to see." Where he got the phrase I do not know, but he liked it, and was always repeating it. However, I had no external evidence that it was he who was my enemy, and I held my peace. I was supported at the public meeting by a speaker from the body of the hall whom I had never seen before. He spoke remarkably well, was evidently educated, and I was rather curious about him.

It was my custom on Saturdays to go out for the whole of the day by the river, seawards, to prepare for the Sunday. I was coming home rather tired, when I met this same man against a stile. He bade me good evening, and then proceeded to thank me for my speech, saying many complimentary things about it. I asked who it was to whom I

had the honour of talking, and he told me he was
Edward Gibbon Mardon. " It was Edward Gibson
Mardon once, sir," he said smilingly. " Gibson was
the name of a rich old aunt who was expected to do
something for me, but I disliked her and never went
near her. I did not see why I should be ticketed
with her label, and as Edward Gibson was very
much like Edward Gibbon, the immortal author of
the 'Decline and Fall,' I dropped the 's' and stuck
in a 'b.' I am nothing but a compositor on the
Sentinel, and Saturday afternoon, after the paper is
out, is a holiday for me, unless there is any report-
ing to do, for I have to turn my attention to that
occasionally." Mr. Edward Gibbon Mardon, I
observed, was slightly built, rather short, and had
scanty whiskers which developed into a little thicker
tuft on his chin. His eyes were pure blue, like the
blue of the speedwell. They were not piercing but
perfectly transparent, indicative of a character which,
if it possessed no particular creative power, would
not permit self-deception. They were not the eyes of
a prophet, but of a man who would not be satisfied
with letting a half-known thing alone and saying
he believed it. His lips were thin, but not compressed into bitterness; and above everything there
was in his face a perfectly legible frankness, con-
trasting pleasantly with the doubtfulness of most of

the faces I know. I expressed my gratitude to him for his kind opinion, and as we loitered he said—

"Sorry to see that attack upon you in the *Sentinel*. I suppose you are aware it was Snale's. Everybody could tell that who knows the man."

"If it is Mr. Snale's, I am very sorry."

"It is Snale's. He is a contemptible cur, and yet it is not his fault. He has heard sermons about all sorts of supernatural subjects for thirty years, and he has never once been warned against meanness, so of course he supposes that supernatural subjects are everything and meanness is nothing. But I will not detain you any longer now, for you are busy. Good-night, sir."

This was rather abrupt and disappointing. However, I was much absorbed in the morrow, and passed on.

Although I despised Snale, his letter was the beginning of a great trouble to me. I had now been preaching for many months, and had met with no response whatever. Occasionally a stranger or two visited the chapel, and with what eager eyes did I not watch for them on the next Sunday, but none of them came twice. It was amazing to me that I could pour out myself as I did, poor although I knew that self to be, and yet make so little impression. Not one man or woman seemed any different

for my being there, and not a soul kindled at any
word of mine, no matter with what earnestness it
might be charged. How I groaned over my incapa-
city to stir in my people any participation in my
thoughts or care for them! Looking at the history
of those days now from a distance of years, everything assumes its proper proportion. I was at work,
it is true, amongst those who were exceptionally
hard and worldly, but I was seeking amongst men
(to put it in orthodox language) what I ought to
have sought with God alone. In other, and perhaps
plainer phrase, I was expecting from men a sympathy which proceeds from the Invisible only; sometimes, indeed, manifesting itself in the long-postponed
justice of time, but more frequently it is nothing
more and nothing less than a consciousness of
approval by the Unseen, a peace unspeakable, which
is bestowed on us when self is suppressed. I
did not know then how little one man can change
another, and what immense and persistent efforts
are necessary—efforts which seldom succeed except
in childhood—in accomplishing anything but the
most superficial alteration of character. Stories are
told of sudden conversions, and of course if a poor
simple creature can be brought to believe that hell-fire
awaits him as the certain penalty of his misdeeds,
he will cease to do them, but this is no real conver-

sion, for essentially he remains pretty much the same kind of being that he was before.

I remember while this mood was on me; that I was much struck with the absolute loneliness of Jesus, and with His horror of that death upon the cross. He was young and full of enthusiastic hope, but when He died He had found hardly anything but misunderstanding. He had written nothing, so that He could not expect that His life would live after Him. Nevertheless His confidence in His own errand had risen so high, that He had not hesitated to proclaim Himself the Messiah: not the Messiah the Jews were expecting, but still the Messiah. I dreamed over His walks by the lake, over the deeper solitude of His last visit to Jerusalem, and over the gloom of that awful Friday afternoon. The hold which He has upon us is easily explained, apart from the dignity of His recorded sayings and the purity of His life. There is no Saviour for us like the hero who has passed triumphantly through the distress which troubles *us*. Salvation is the spectacle of a victory by another over foes like our own. The story of Jesus is the story of the poor and forgotten. He is not the Saviour for the rich and prosperous, for they want no Saviour. The healthy, active, and well-to-do need Him not, and require nothing more than is given by their own health and prosperity.

But every one who has walked in sadness because his destiny has not fitted his aspirations; every one who, having no opportunity to lift himself out of his little narrow town or village circle of acquaintances, has thirsted for something beyond what they could give him; everybody who, with nothing but a dull, daily round of mechanical routine before him, would welcome death, if it were martyrdom for a cause; every humblest creature, in the obscurity of great cities or remote hamlets, who silently does his or her duty without recognition— all these turn to Jesus, and find themselves in Him. He died, faithful to the end, with infinitely higher hopes, purposes, and capacity than mine, and with almost no promise of anything to come of them.

Something of this kind I preached one Sunday, more as a relief to myself than for any other reason. Mardon was there, and with him a girl whom I had not seen before. My sight is rather short, and I could not very well tell what she was like. After the service was over he waited for me, and said he had done so to ask me if I would pay him a visit on Monday evening. I promised to do so, and accordingly went. I found him living in a small brick-built cottage near the outskirts of the town, the rental of which I should suppose would be about

seven or eight pounds a year. There was a patch
of ground in front and a little garden behind, a
kind of narrow strip about fifty feet long separated
from the other little strips by iron hurdles. Mardon
had tried to keep his garden in order and had succeeded, but his neighbour was disorderly, and had
allowed weeds to grow, blacking bottles and old
tin cans to accumulate, so that whatever pleasure
Mardon's labours might have afforded was somewhat
spoiled. He himself came to the door when I
knocked, and I was shown into a kind of sitting-
room with a round table in the middle and furnished
with windsor chairs, two arm-chairs of the same
kind standing on either side the fireplace. Against
the window was a smaller table with a green baize
tablecloth, and about half-a-dozen plants stood on
the window-sill serving as a screen. In the recess
on one side of the fireplace was a cupboard, upon
the top of which stood a teacaddy, a workbox, some
tumblers, and a decanter full of water; the other
side being filled with a bookcase and books. There
were two or three pictures on the walls; one was a
portrait of Voltaire, another of Lord Bacon, and a
third was Albert Dürer's St. Jerome. This latter was
an heirloom, and greatly prized I could perceive, as
it was hung in the place of honour over the mantelpiece. After some little introductory talk, the same

girl whom I had noticed with Mardon at the chapel came in, and I was introduced to her as his only daughter Mary. She began to busy herself at once in getting the tea. She was under the average height for a woman, and delicately built. Her head was small, but the neck was long. Her hair was brown of a peculiarly lustrous tint, partly due to nature, but also to a looseness of arrangement and a most diligent use of the brush, so that the light fell not upon a dead compact mass, but upon myriads of individual hairs, each of which reflected the light. Her eyes, so far as I could make out, were a kind of greenish grey, but the eyelashes were long, so that it was difficult exactly to discover what was underneath them. The hands were small, and the whole figure exquisitely graceful; the plain black dress, which she wore fastened right up to the throat, suiting her to perfection. Her face, as I first thought, did not seem indicative of strength. The lips were thin but not straight, the upper lip showing a remarkable curve in it. Nor was it a handsome face. The complexion was not sufficiently transparent, nor were the features regular. During tea she spoke very little, but I noticed one peculiarity about her manner of talking, and that was its perfect simplicity. There was no sort of effort or strain in anything she said, no attempt by emphasis of words to

make up for weakness of thought, and no compliance
with that vulgar and most disagreeable habit of using
intense language to describe what is not intense in
itself. Her yea was yea, and her no, no. I observed
also that she spoke without disguise, although she
was not rude. The manners of the cultivated classes
are sometimes very charming, and more particularly
their courtesy, which puts the guest so much at his
ease, and constrains him to believe that an almost
personal interest is taken in his affairs, but after a
time it becomes wearisome. It is felt to be nothing
but courtesy, the result of a rule of conduct uniform
for all, and verging very closely upon hypocrisy.
We long rather for plainness of speech, for some
intimation of the person with whom we are talking,
and that the mask and gloves may be laid aside. Tea
being over, Miss Mardon cleared away the tea things,
and presently came back again. She took one of the
arm-chairs by the side of the fireplace, which her father
had reserved for her, and while he and I were talking,
she sat with her head leaning a little sideways on the
back of the chair. I could just discern that her feet,
which rested on the stool, were very diminutive, like
her hands. The talk with Mardon turned upon the
chapel. I had begun it by saying that I had noticed
him there on the Sunday just mentioned. He then
explained why he never went to any place of worship.

A purely orthodox preacher it was, of course, impossible for him to hear, but beyond that he doubted the efficacy of preaching. What could be the use of it, supposing the preacher no longer to be a believer in the common creeds? If he turns himself into a mere lecturer on all sorts of topics, he does nothing more than books do, and they do it much better. He must base himself upon the Bible, and above all upon Christ, and how can he base himself upon a myth? We do not know that Christ ever lived, or that if He lived His life was anything like what is attributed to Him. A mere juxtaposition of the gospels shows how the accounts of His words and deeds differ according to the tradition followed by each of His biographers. I interrupted Mardon at this point by saying that it did not matter whether Christ actually existed or not. What the four evangelists recorded was eternally true, and the Christ-idea was true whether it was ever incarnated or not in a being bearing His name. "Pardon me," said Mardon, "but it does very much matter. It is all the matter whether we are dealing with a dream or with reality. I can dream about a man's dying on the cross in homage to what he believed, but I would not perhaps die there myself; and when I suffer from hesitation whether I ought to sacrifice myself for the truth, it is of

E

immense assistance to me to know that a greater sacrifice has been made before me—that a greater sacrifice is possible. To know that somebody has poetically imagined that it is possible, and has very likely been altogether incapable of its achievement, is no help. Moreover, the commonplaces which even the most freethinking of Unitarians seem to consider as axiomatic, are to me far from certain, and even unthinkable. For example, they are always talking about the omnipotence of God. But power even of the supremest kind necessarily implies an object—that is to say, resistance. Without an object which resists it, it would be a blank, and what then is the meaning of omnipotence? It is not that it is merely inconceivable; it is nonsense, and so are all these abstract, illimitable, self-annihilative attributes of which God is made up."

This negative criticism, in which Mardon greatly excelled, was all new to me, and I had no reply to make. He had a sledge-hammer way of expressing himself, while I, on the contrary, always required time to bring into shape what I saw. Just then I saw nothing; I was stunned, bewildered, out of the sphere of my own thoughts, and pained at the roughness with which he treated what I had cherished. I was presently relieved, however, of further reflection by Mardon's asking his daughter

whether her face was better. It turned out that all
the afternoon and evening she had suffered greatly
from neuralgia. She had said nothing about it
while I was there, although she had behaved with
cheerfulness and freedom. Mentally I had accused
her of slightness, and inability to talk upon the subjects which interested Mardon and myself; but when
I·knew she had been in torture all the time, my
opinion was altered. I thought how rash I had been
in judging her as I continually judged other people,
without being aware of everything they had to pass
through; and I thought, too, that if I had a fit of
neuralgia, everybody near me would know it, and be
almost as much annoyed by me as I myself should
be by the pain. It is curious, also, that when thus
proclaiming my troubles I often considered my
eloquence meritorious, or, at least, a kind of talent
for which I ought to praise God, contemning rather
my silent friends as something nearer than myself
to the expressionless animals. To parade my tooth-
ache, describing it with unusual adjectives, making it
felt by all the company in which I might happen to
be, was to me an assertion of my superior nature.
But, looking at Mary, and thinking about her as I
walked home, I perceived that her ability to be
quiet, to subdue herself, to resist the temptation for
a whole evening of drawing attention to herself by

telling us what she was enduring, was heroism, and that my contrary tendency was pitiful vanity. I perceived that such virtues as patience and self-denial —which, clad in russet dress, I had often passed by unnoticed when I had found them amongst the poor or the humble—were more precious and more ennobling to their possessor than poetic yearnings, or the power to propound rhetorically to the world my grievances or agonies.

Miss Mardon's face was getting worse, and as by this time it was late, I stayed but a little while longer.

CHAPTER V.

MISS ARBOUR.

For some months I continued without much change in my monotonous existence. I did not see Mardon often, for I rather dreaded him. I could not resist him, and I shrank from what I saw to be inevitably true when I talked to him. I can hardly say it was cowardice. Those may call it cowardice to whom all associations are nothing, and to whom beliefs are no more than matters of indifferent research; but as for me, Mardon's talk darkened my days and nights. I never could understand the light manner in which people will discuss the gravest questions, such as God, and the immortality of the soul. They gossip about them over their tea, write and read review articles about them, and seem to consider affirmation or negation of no more practical importance than the conformation of a beetle. With me the struggle to retain as much as I could of my creed was tremendous. The dissolution of Jesus into mythologic vapour was nothing less than the death of a friend dearer to me then than any other friend whom I knew. But the worst stroke of all was that which fell upon the doctrine of a life beyond the grave. In theory I had long despised the notion that we should govern our conduct here by hope of reward or fear of punishment hereafter. But under Mardon's remorseless criticism, when he insisted on asking for the where and how, and on pointing out that all attempts to say where and how ended in nonsense, my hope began to fail, and I was surprised to find myself incapable of living with proper serenity if there was nothing but blank darkness before me at the end of a few years. As I got older I became aware of the folly of this perpetual reaching after the future, and of drawing from to-morrow, and from to-morrow only, a reason for the joyfulness of to-day. I learned, when, alas! it was almost too late, to live in each moment as it passed over my head, believing that the sun as it is now rising is as good as it will ever be, and blinding myself as much as possible to what may follow. But when I was young I was the victim of that illusion, implanted for some purpose or other in us by Nature, which causes us, on the brightest morning in June, to think immediately of a brighter morning which is to come in July. I say nothing, now, for or against the doctrine of immortality. All I say is, that men have been happy without it, even under the pressure of disaster, and that to make immortality a sole spring of action here, is an exaggeration of the folly which deludes us all through life with endless expectation, and leaves us at death without the thorough enjoyment of a single hour.

So I shrank from Mardon, but none the less did the process of excavation go on. It often happens that a man loses faith without knowing it. Silently the foundation is sapped while the building stands fronting the sun, as solid to all appearance as when it was first turned out of the builder's hands, but at last it falls suddenly with a crash. It was so at this time with a personal relationship of mine, about which I have hitherto said nothing. Years ago, before I went to college, and when I was a teacher in the Sunday school, I had fallen in love with one of my fellow-teachers, and we became engaged. She was the daughter of one of the deacons. She had a smiling, pretty, vivacious face; was always somehow foremost in school treats, picnics and chapel-work, and she had a kind of piquant manner, which to many men is more ensnaring than beauty. She never read anything; she was too restless and fond of outward activity for that, and no questions about orthodoxy or heresy ever troubled her head. We continued our correspondence regularly after my appointment as minister, and her friends, I knew, were looking to me to fix a day for marriage. But although we had been writing to one another as affectionately as usual, a revolution had taken place. I was quite unconscious of it, for we had been betrothed for so long that I never once considered the possibility of any rupture. One Monday morning, however, I had a letter from her. It was not often that she wrote on Sunday, as she had a religious prejudice against writing letters on that day. However, this was urgent, for it was to tell me that an aunt of hers who was staying at her father's was just dead, and that her uncle wanted her to go and live with him for sometime, to look after the little children who were left behind. She said that her dear aunt died a beautiful death, trusting in the merits of the Redeemer. She also added, in a very delicate way, that she would have agreed to go to her uncle's at once, but she had understood that we were to be married soon, and she did not like to leave home for long. She was evidently anxious for me to tell her what to do. This letter, as I have said, came to me on Monday, when I was exhausted by a more than usually desolate Sunday. I became at once aware that my affection for her, if it ever really existed, had departed. I saw before me the long days of wedded life with no sympathy, and I shuddered when I thought what I should do with such a wife. How could I take her to Mardon? how could I ask him to come to me? Strange to say, my pride suffered most. I could have endured, I believe, even discord at home, if only I could have had a woman whom I could present to my friends, and whom they would admire. I was never unselfish in the way in which women are, and yet I have always been more anxious that people should respect my wife than respect me, and at any time would withdraw myself into the shade if only she might be brought into the light. This is nothing noble. It is an obscure form of egotism probably, but anyhow, such always was my case. It took but a very few hours to excite me to distraction. I had gone on for years without realising what I saw now, and although in the situation itself the change had been only gradual, it instantaneously became intolerable. Yet I never was more incapable of acting. What could I do? After such a long betrothal, to break loose from her would be cruel and shameful. I could never hold up my head again, and in the narrow circle of Independency, the whole affair would be, known and my prospects ruined. Then other and subtler reasons presented themselves. No men can expect ideal attachments. We must be satisfied with ordinary humanity. Doubtless my friend with a lofty imagination would be better matched with some Antigone who exists somewhere and whom he does not know. But he wisely does not spend his life in vain search after her, but settles down with the first decently sensible woman he finds in his own street, and makes the best of his bargain. Besides, there was the power of use and wont to be considered. Ellen had no vice of temper, no meanness, and it was not improbable that she would be just as good a helpmeet for me in time as I had a right to ask. Living together we should mould one another, and at last like one another. Marrying her, I should be relieved from the insufferable solitude which was depressing me to death, and should have a home. So it has always been with me. When there has been the sternest need of promptitude, I have seen such multitudes of arguments for and against every course that I have despaired. I have at my command any number of maxims, all of them good, but I am powerless to select the one which ought to be applied. A general principle, a fine saying, is nothing but a tool, and the wit of man is shown not in his possession of a well-furnished tool chest, but in the ability to pick out the proper instrument and use it. I remained in this miserable condition for days, not venturing to answer Ellen's letter, until at last I

turned out for a walk. I have often found that
motion and change will bring light and resolution
when thinking will not. I started off in the morning down by the river, and towards the sea, my
favourite stroll. I went on and on under a leaden
sky, through the level, solitary, marshy meadows,
where the river began to lose itself in the ocean, and
I wandered about there, struggling for guidance. In
my distress I actually knelt down and prayed, but
the heavens remained impassive as before, and I was
half ashamed of what I had done, as if it were a
piece of hypocrisy. At last, wearied out, I turned
homeward, and diverging from the direct road I was
led past the house where the Misses Arbour lived.
I was faint, and some beneficent inspiration prompted
me to call. I went in, and found that the younger
of the two sisters was out. A sudden tendency to
hysterics overcame me, and I asked for a glass of water.
Miss Arbour, having given it to me, sat down on the
side of the fireplace opposite to the one at which I was
sitting, and for a few moments there was silence. I
made some commonplace observation, but instead of
answering me she said quietly, " Mr. Rutherford,
you have been upset; I hope you have met with no
accident." How it come about I do not know, but
my whole story rushed to my lips, and I told her all
of it with quivering voice. I cannot imagine what

possessed me to make her my confidante. Shy, reserved, and proud, I would have died rather than have breathed a syllable of my secret if I had been in my ordinary humour, but her soft, sweet face altogether overpowered me. As I proceeded with my tale, the change that came over her was most remarkable. When I began she was leaning back placidly in her large chair, with her handkerchief upon her lap; but gradually her face kindled, she sat upright, and she was transformed with a completeness and suddenness which I could not have conceived possible. At last, when I had finished, she put both her hands to her forehead, and almost shrieked out, "Shall I tell him?—O my God, shall I tell him?—may God have mercy on him." I was amazed beyond measure at the altogether unsuspected depth of passion which was revealed in her whom I had never before seen disturbed by more than a ripple of emotion. She drew her chair nearer to mine, put both her hands on my knees, looked right into my eyes, and said, "Listen." She then moved back a little, and spoke as follows:—

"It is forty-five years ago this month since I was married. You are surprised; you have always known me under my maiden name, and you thought I had always been single. It is forty-six years ago this month since the man who afterwards became

my husband first saw me. He was partner in a
cloth firm. At that time it was the duty of one
member of a firm to travel, and he came to our town,
where my father was a well-to-do carriage-builder.
My father was an old customer of his house, and the
relationship between the customer and the whole-
sale merchant was then very different to what it is
now. Consequently, Mr. Hexton, for that was my
husband's name, was continually asked to stay with
us so long as he remained in the town. He was
what might be called a singularly handsome man,
that is to say, he was upright, well made, with a
straight nose, black hair, dark eyes, and a good complexion. He dressed with perfect neatness and good
taste, and had the reputation of being a most temperate and most moral man, much respected amongst
the sect to which both of us belonged. When he
first came our way I was about nineteen and he
about three-and-twenty. My father and his had
long been acquainted, and he was of course received
even with cordiality. I was excitable, a lover of
poetry, a reader of all sorts of books, and much
given to enthusiasm. Ah! you do not think so, you
do not see how that can have been, but you do not
know how unaccountable is the development of the
soul, and what is the meaning of any given form of
character which presents itself to you. You see

nothing but the peaceful, long since settled result,
but how it came there, what its history has been, you
cannot tell.   It may always have been there, or
have gradually grown so, in gradual progress from
seed to flower, or it may be the final repose of tremendous forces. . I will show you what I was like
at nineteen," and she got up and turned to a desk, from
which she took a little ivory miniature. "That," she
said, "was given to Mr. Hexton when we were engaged.
I thought he would have locked it up, but he used to
leave it about, and one day I found it in the dressing-
table drawer, with some brushes and combs, and two
or three letters of mine. I withdrew it, and burnt the
letters. He never asked for it, and here it is." The
head was small and set upon the neck like a flower,
but not bending pensively. It was rather thrown
back with a kind of firmness, and with a peculiarly
open air, as if it had nothing to conceal and wished
the world to conceal nothing. The body was shown
down to the waist, and was slim and graceful.
But what was most noteworthy about the picture
was its solemn seriousness, a seriousness capable of
infinite affection, and of infinite abandonment, not
sensuous abandonment—everything was too severe,
too much controlled by the arch of the top of the
head for that—but of an abandonment to spiritual
aims. Miss Arbour continued: "Mr. Hexton after

a while gave me to understand that he was my
admirer, and before six months of acquaintanceship
had passed my mother told me that he had requested
formally that he might be considered as my suitor.
She put no pressure upon me, nor did my father,
excepting that they said that if I would accept Mr.
Hexton they would be content, as they knew him to
be a very well-conducted young man, a member of
the church, and prosperous in his business. My
first, and for a time my sovereign, impulse was to
reject him, because I thought him mean, and because
I felt he lacked sympathy with me. Unhappily I
did not trust that impulse. I looked for something
more authoritative, but I was mistaken, for the
voice of God, to me at least, hardly ever comes in
thunder, but I have to listen with perfect stillness
to make it out. It spoke to me, told me what to
do, but I argued with it and was lost. I was guilt-
less of any base motive, but I found the wrong name
for what displeased me in Mr. Hexton, and so I
deluded myself. I reasoned that his meanness was
justifiable economy, and that his dissimilarity from
me was perhaps the very thing which ought to
induce me to marry him, because he would correct
my failings. I knew I was too inconsiderate, too
rash, too flighty, and I said to myself that his
soberness would be a good thing for me. Oh, if I

had but the power to write a book which should go to the ends of the world, and warn young men and women not to be led away by any sophistry when choosing their partners for life! It may be asked, How are we to distinguish heavenly instigation from hellish temptation? I say, that neither you nor I, sitting here, can tell how to do it. We can lay down no law by which infallibly to recognise the messenger from God. But what I do say is, that when the moment comes, it is perfectly easy for us to recognise him. Whether we listen to his message or not is another matter. If we do not—if we stop to dispute with him, we are undone, for we shall very soon learn to discredit him. So I was married, and I went to live in a dark manufacturing town, away from all my friends. I awoke to my misery by degrees, but still rapidly. I had my books sent down to me. I unpacked them in Mr. Hexton's presence, and I kindled at the thought of ranging my old favourites in my sitting-room. He saw my delight as I put them on some empty shelves, but the next day he said that he wanted a stuffed dog there, and that he thought my books, especially as they were shabby, had better go upstairs. We had to give some entertainments soon afterwards. The minister and his wife, with some other friends, came to tea, and the conversation turned on parties

and the dulness of winter evenings if no amusements
were provided. I maintained that rational human
beings ought not to be dependent upon childish
games, but ought to be able to occupy themselves
and interest themselves with talk. Talk, I said,—
not gossip but talk pleases me better than chess
or forfeits; and the lines of Cowper occurred to me—

'When one, that holds communion with the skies,
 Has filled his urn where these pure waters rise,
 And once more mingles with us meaner things,
 'Tis even as if an angel shook his wings ;
 Immortal fragrance fills the circuit wide,
 That tells us whence his treasures are supplied.'

I ventured to repeat this verse, and when I had
finished, there was a pause for a moment, which was
broken by my husband's saying to the minister's
wife, who sat next to him, 'O Mrs. Cook, I quite
forgot to express my sympathy with you; I heard
that you had lost your cat.' The blow was delibe-
rately administered, and I felt it as an insult. I was
wrong, I know. I was ignorant of the ways of the
world, and I ought to have been aware of the
folly of placing myself above the level of my
guests, and of the extreme unwisdom of revealing
myself in that unguarded way to strangers. Two or
three more experiences of that kind taught me to
close myself carefully to all the world, and to beware

F

how I uttered anything more than commonplace.
But I was young, and ought to have been pardoned.
I felt the sting of self-humiliation far into the
night, as I lay and silently cried, while Mr. Hexton
slept beside me. I soon found that he was entirely
insensible to everything for which I most cared.
Before our marriage he had affected a sort of interest
in my pursuits, but in reality he was indifferent
to them. He was cold, hard, and impenetrable.
His habits were precise and methodical, beyond
what is natural for a man of his years. I remember
one evening—strange that these small events should
so burn themselves into me—that some friends
were at our house to tea. A tradesman in the
town was mentioned, a member of our congregation,
who had become bankrupt, and everybody began
to abuse him. It was said that he had been extra-
vagant; that he had chosen to send his children to
the grammar-school, where the children of gentlefolk
went; and finally, that only last year he had let his
wife go to the seaside. I knew what the real state
of affairs was. He had perhaps been living a little
beyond his means, but as to the school, he had
rather refined tastes, and he longed to teach his
children something more than the ciphering, as it
was called, and bookkeeping which they would have
learned at the academy at which men in his position

usually educated their boys; and as to the seaside, his wife was ill, and he could not bear to see her suffering in the smoky street, when he knew that a little fresh air and change of scene would restore her. So I said that I was sorry to hear the poor man attacked; that he had done wrong, no doubt, but so had the woman who was brought before Jesus; and that with me, charity or a large heart covered a multitude of sins. I added that there was something dreadful in the way in which everybody always seemed to agree in deserting the unfortunate. I was a little moved, and unluckily upset a teacup. No harm was done; and if my husband, who sat next to me, had chosen to take no notice, there need have been no disturbance whatever. But he made a great fuss, crying, 'Oh, my dear, pray mind! Ring the bell instantly, or it will all be through the tablecloth.' In getting up hastily to obey him, I happened to drag the cloth, as it lay on my lap; a plate fell down and was broken; everything was in confusion; I was ashamed and degraded.

"I do not believe there was a single point in Mr. Hexton's character in which he touched the universal; not a single chink, however narrow, through which his soul looked out of itself upon the great world around. If he had kept bees, or collected butterflies or beetles, I could have found some avenue of approach. But he had no taste for anything of the kind. He had his breakfast at eight regularly every morning, and read his letters at breakfast. He came home to dinner at two, looked at the newspaper for a little while after dinner, and then he would go to sleep. At six he had his tea, and in half an hour went back to his counting-house, which he did not leave till eight. Supper at nine, and bed at ten, closed the day. It was a habit of mine to read a little after supper, and occasionally I read aloud to him passages which struck me, but I soon gave it up, for once or twice he said to me, 'Now you've got to the bottom of that page, I think you had better go to bed,' although perhaps the page did not end a sentence. But why weary you with all this? I pass over all the rest of the hateful details which made life insupportable to me. Suffice to say, that one wet Sunday evening, when we could not go to chapel and were in the dining-room alone, the climax was reached. My husband had a religious magazine before him, and I sat still doing nothing. At last, after an hour had passed without a word, I could bear it no longer, and I broke out—

"'James, I am wretched beyond description!'

"He slowly shut the magazine, tearing a piece of paper from a letter and putting it in as a mark, and then said—

" ' What is the matter ? '

" ' You must know. You must know that ever since we have been married you have never cared for one single thing I have done or said, that is to say, you have never cared for me. It is *not* being married.'

" It was an explosive outburst, sudden and almost incoherent, and I cried as if my heart would break.

" ' What is the meaning of all this? You must be unwell. Will you not have a glass of wine ? '

" I could not regain myself for some minutes, during which he sat perfectly still, without speaking, and without touching me. His coldness nerved me again, congealing all my emotion into a set resolve, and I said—

" ' I want no wine. I am not unwell. I do not wish to have a scene. I will not, by useless words, embitter myself against you, or you against me. You know you do not love me. I know I do not love you. It is all a bitter, cursed mistake, and the sooner we say so and rectify it the better.'

" The colour left his face ; his lips quivered, and he looked as if he would have killed me.

" ' What monstrous thing is this? What do you mean by your tomfooleries ? '

" I did not speak.

"'Speak,' he roared. 'What am I to understand by rectifying your mistake? By the living God, you shall not make me the laughing-stock and gossip of the town. I'll crush you first.'

"I was astonished to see such rage develop itself so suddenly in him, and yet afterwards, when I came to reflect, I saw there was no reason for surprise. Self, self was his god, and the thought of the damage which would be done to him and his reputation was what roused him. I was still silent, and he went on—

"'I suppose you intend to leave me, and you think you'll disgrace me. You'll disgrace yourself. Everybody knows me here, and knows you've had every comfort and everything to make you happy. Everybody will say what everybody will have the right to say about you. Out with it and confess the truth, that one of your snivelling poets has fallen in love with you and you with him.'

"I still held my peace, but I rose and went into the best bedchamber, and sat there in the dark till bedtime. I heard James come upstairs at ten o'clock as usual, go to his own room and lock himself in. I never hesitated a moment. I could not go home to become the centre of all the chatter of the little provincial town in which I was born. My old nurse, who took care of me as a child, had got a place in London as housekeeper in a large shop in the Strand.

She was always very fond of me, and to her instantly
I determined to go. I came down, wrote a brief
note to James, stating that after his base and lying
sneer he could not expect to find me in the morning still with him, and telling him I had left him
for ever. I put on my cloak, took some money
which was my own out of my cashbox, and at half-
past twelve heard the mail-coach approaching. I
opened the front door softly—it shut with an oiled
spring bolt; I went out, stopped the coach, and was
presently rolling over the road to the great city.
Oh that night! I was the sole passenger inside, and
for some hours I remained stunned, hardly knowing
what had become of me. Soon the morning began
to break, with such calm and such slow changing
splendour that it drew me out of myself to look at
it, and it seemed to me a prophecy of the future.
No words can tell the bound of my heart at eman-
cipation. I did not know what was before me, but
I knew from what I had escaped; I did not believe
I should be pursued, and no sailor returning from
shipwreck and years of absence ever entered the port
where wife and children were with more rapture
than I felt journeying through the rain into which
the clouds of the sunrise dissolved, as we rode over the
dim flats of Huntingdonshire southwards. There is
no need for me to weary you any longer, nor to tell

you what happened after I got to London, or how I came here. I had a little property of my own, and no child. To avoid questions I resumed my maiden name. But one thing you must know, because it will directly tend to enforce what I am going to beseech of you. Years afterwards, I might have married a man who was devoted to me. But I told him I was married already, and not a word of love must he speak to me. He went abroad in despair, and I have never seen anything more of him.

"You can guess now what I am going to pray of you to do. Without hesitation, write to this girl and tell her the exact truth. Anything; any obloquy; anything friends or enemies may say of you must be faced even joyfully, rather than what I had to endure. Better die the death of the Saviour on the cross than live such a life as mine."

I said: "Miss Arbour, you are doubtless right, but think what it means. It means nothing less than infamy. It will be said, I broke the poor thing's heart, and marred her prospects for ever. What will become of me, as a minister, when all this is known?"

She caught my hand in hers, and cried with indescribable feeling—

"My good sir, you are parleying with the great Enemy of Souls. Oh, if you did but know, if you *could* but know, you would be as decisive in your

recoil from him, as you would from hell suddenly
opened at your feet. Never mind the future. The
one thing you have to do is the thing that lies next
to you, divinely ordained for you. What does the
119th Psalm say? 'Thy word is a lamp unto my feet.'
We have no light promised us to show us our road
a hundred miles away, but we have a light for the
next footstep, and if we take that, we shall have a
light for the one which is to follow. The inspiration
of the Almighty could not make clearer to me the
message I deliver to you. Forgive me—you are a
minister, I know, and perhaps I ought not to speak
so to you, but I am an old woman. Never would
you have heard my history from me, if I had not
thought it would help to save you from something
worse than death."

At this moment there came a knock at the door,
and Miss Arbour's sister came in. After a few
words of greeting I took my leave and walked home.
I was confounded. Who could have dreamed that
such tragic depths lay behind that serene face, and
that her orderly precision was like the grass and
flowers upon volcanic soil with Vesuvian fires slum-
bering below? I had been altogether at fault, and I
was taught, what I have since been taught over and
over again, that unknown abysses, into which the
sun never shines, lie covered with commonplace

in men and women, and are revealed only by the rarest opportunity.

But my thoughts turned almost immediately to myself, and I could bring myself to no resolve. I was weak and tired, and the more I thought the less capable was I of coming to any decision. In the morning, after a restless night, I was in still greater straits, and being perfectly unable to do anything, I fled to my usual refuge, the sea. The whole day I swayed to and fro, without the smallest power to arbitrate between the contradictory impulses which drew me in opposite directions. I knew what I ought to do, but Ellen's image was ever before me, mutely appealing against her wrongs, and I pictured her deserted and with her life spoiled. I said to myself that instinct is all very well, but for what purpose is reason given to us if not to reason with it; and reasoning in the main is a correction of what is called instinct and of hasty first impressions. I knew many cases in which men and women loved one another without similarity of opinions, and after all, similarity of opinions upon theological criticism is a poor bond of union. But then, no sooner was this pleaded than the other side of the question was propounded with all its distinctness, as Miss Arbour had presented it. I came home thoroughly beaten with fatigue, and went to bed.

Fortunately I sank at once to rest, and with the morning was born the clear discernment that whatever I ought to do, it was more manly of me to go than to write to Ellen. Accordingly, I made arrangements for getting somebody to supply my place in the pulpit for a couple of Sundays, and went home.

CHAPTER VI.

ELLEN AND MARY.

I NOW found myself in the strangest position. What was I to do? Was I to go to Ellen at once and say plainly, "I have ceased to care for you?" I did what all weak people do. I wished that destiny would take the matter out of my hands. I would have given the world if I could have heard that Ellen was fonder of somebody else than me, although the moment the thought came to me I saw its baseness. But destiny was determined to try me to the uttermost, and make the task as difficult for me as it could be made. It was Thursday when I arrived, and somehow or other— how I do not know—I found myself on Thursday afternoon at her house. She was very pleased to see me, for many reasons. My last letters had been doubtful, and the time for our marriage, as she at least thought, was at hand. I, on my part, could not but return the usual embrace, but after the first few words were over there was a silence, and she

noticed that I did not look well. Anxiously she
asked me what was the matter. I said that something had been upon my mind for a long time,
which I thought it my duty to tell her. I then
went on to say that I felt she ought to know what
had happened. When we were first engaged we
both professed the same faith. From that faith I
had gradually departed, and it seemed to me that
it would be wicked if she were not made acquainted
before she took a step which was irrevocable. This
was true, but it was not quite all the truth, and
with a woman's keenness she saw at once everything
that was in me. She broke out instantly with a sob.
"O Rough!" a nickname she had given me, "I
know what it all means—you want to get rid of me."

God help me, if I ever endure greater anguish
than I did then. I could not speak, much less
could I weep, and I sat and watched her for some
minutes in silence. My first impulse was to retract,
to put my arms round her neck, and swear that
whatever I might be, Deist or Atheist, nothing
should separate me from her. Old associations, the
thought of the cruel injustice put upon her, the dis-
play of an emotion which I had never seen in her
before, almost overmastered me, and why I did not
yield I do not know. Again and again have I
failed to make out what it is which, in moments of

extreme peril, has restrained me from making some deadly mistake, when I have not been aware of the conscious exercise of any authority of my own. At last I said—

"Ellen, what else was I to do? I cannot help my conversion to another creed. Supposing you had found out that you had married a Unitarian and I had never told you!"

"O Rough! you are not a Unitarian, you don't love me," and she sobbed afresh.

I could not plead against hysterics. I was afraid she would get ill. I thought nobody was in the house, and I rushed across the passage to get her some stimulants. When I came back her father was in the room. He was my aversion—a fussy, conceited man, who always prated about " my daughter" to me in a tone which was very repulsive—just as if she were his property, and he were her natural protector against me.

" Mr. Rutherford," he cried, "what is the matter with my daughter? What have you said to her?"

" I don't think, sir, I am bound to tell you. It is a matter between Ellen and myself."

" Mr. Rutherford, I demand an explanation. Ellen is mine. I am her father."

" Excuse me, sir, if I desire not to have a scene here just now. Ellen is unwell. When she recovers she will tell you. I had better leave," and I walked straight out of the house, never to enter it again.

Next morning I had a letter from her father to say, that whether I was a Unitarian or not my behaviour to Ellen showed I was bad enough to be one. Anyhow, he had forbidden her all further intercourse with me. I went back home, and never heard from her again. When I had once more settled down in my solitude, and came to think over what had happened, I felt the self-condemnation of a criminal without being able to accuse myself of a crime. I believe with Miss Arbour that it is madness for a young man who finds out he has made a blunder, not to set it right; no matter what the wrench may be. But that Ellen was a victim I do not deny. If any sin, however, was committed against her, it was committed long before our separation. It was nine-tenths mistake and one-tenth something more heinous, and the worst of it is, that while there is nothing which a man does which is of greater consequence than the choice of a woman with whom he is to live, there is nothing he does in which he is more liable to self-deception.

On my return I heard that Mardon was ill, and that probably he would die. During my absence a contested election for the county had taken place, and our town was one of the polling places. The lower classes were violently Tory. During the excitement of the contest the mob had set upon Mardon as he was going to his work, and had reviled him as a Republican and an Atheist. By way of proving their theism they had cursed him with many oaths, and had so sorely beaten him that the shock was almost fatal. I went to see him instantly, and found him in much pain, believing that he would not get better, but perfectly peaceful. I knew that he had no faith in immortality, and I was curious beyond measure to see how he would encounter death without such a faith; for the problem of death, and of life after death, was still absorbing me even to the point of monomania. I had been struggling as best I could to protect myself against it, but with little success. I had long since seen the absurdity and impossibility of the ordinary theories of hell and heaven. I could not give up my hope in a continuance of life beyond the grave, but the moment I came to ask myself *how*, I was involved in contradictions. Immortality is not really immortality of the person unless the memory abides and there be a connection of the self of the next world with the self here, and it was incredible to me that there should be any memories or any such connection after the dissolution of the body; moreover, the soul, whatever it may be, is so intimately one with the body, and is affected so seriously by the weaknesses, passions, and prejudices of the body, that without it my soul would not be myself, and the fable of the resurrection of the body, of this same brain and heart, was more than I could ever swallow in my most orthodox days. But the greatest difficulty was the inability to believe that the Almighty intended to preserve all the mass of human beings, all the countless millions of barbaric, half-bestial forms which, since the appearance of man. had wandered upon the earth, savage or civilised. Is it like Nature's way to be so careful about individuals, and is it to be supposed that having produced, millions of years ago, a creature scarcely nobler than the animals he tore with his fingers, she should take pains to maintain him in existence for evermore? The law of the universe everywhere, is rather the perpetual rise from the lower to the higher; an immortality of aspiration after more perfect types; a suppression and happy forgetfulness of its comparative failures. There was nevertheless an obstacle to the acceptance of this negation in a faintness of heart which I could not overcome. Why this ceaseless struggle, if in a few short years I was to be asleep for ever? The position of mortal man seemed to me infinitely tragic. He is born into the world, beholds its grandeur and beauty, is filled with unquenchable longings, and knows that in a

few inevitable revolutions of the earth he will cease.
More painful still; he loves somebody, man or woman,
with a surpassing devotion ; he is so lost in his love
that he cannot endure a moment without it; and
when he sees it pass away in death, he is told
that it is extinguished—that that heart and mind
absolutely are *not*. It was always a weakness with
me that certain thoughts preyed on me. I was
always singularly feeble in laying hold of an idea,
and in the ability to compel myself to dwell upon
a thing for any lengthened period in continuous
exhaustive reflection. But, nevertheless, ideas would
frequently lay hold of *me* with such relentless tena-
city that I was passive in their grasp. So it was
about this time with death and immortality, and
I watched eagerly Mardon's behaviour when the end
had to be faced. As I have said, he was altogether
calm. I did not like to question him while he was
so unwell, because I knew that a discussion would
arise which I could not control, and it might
disturb him, but I would have given anything to
understand what was passing in his mind.

During his sickness I was much impressed by
Mary's manner of nursing him. She was always
entirely wrapped up in her father, so much so, that
I had often doubted if she could survive him ; but
she never revealed any trace of agitation. Under

the pressure of the calamity which had befallen her, she showed rather increased steadiness, and even a cheerfulness which surprised me. Nothing went wrong in the house. Everything was perfectly ordered, perfectly quiet, and she rose to a height of which I had never suspected her capable, while her father's stronger nature was allowed to predominate. She was absolutely dependent on him. If he did not get well she would be penniless, and I could not help thinking that with the like chance before me, to say nothing of my love for him and anxiety lest he should die, I should be distracted, and lose my head; more especially if I had to sit by his bed, and spend sleepless nights such as fell to her lot. But she belonged to that class of natures which, although delicate and fragile, rejoice in difficulty. Her grief for her father was exquisite, but it was controlled by a sense of her responsibility. The greater the peril, the more complete was her self-command.

To the surprise of everybody Mardon got better. His temperate habits befriended him in a manner which amazed his more indulgent neighbours, who were accustomed to hot suppers, and whisky and water after them. Meanwhile I fell into greater difficulties than ever in my ministry. I wonder now that I was not stopped earlier. I was entirely unorthodox, through mere powerlessness to believe,

and the catalogue of the articles of faith to which
I might be said really to subscribe was very brief.
I could no longer preach any of the dogmas which
had always been preached in the chapel, and I
strove to avoid a direct conflict by taking Scripture
characters, amplifying them from the hints in the
Bible, and neglecting what was supernatural. That
I was allowed to go on for so long was mainly due
to the isolation of the town and the ignorance of
my hearers. Mardon and his daughter came frequently to hear me, and this I believe finally roused
suspicion more than any doctrine expounded from
the pulpit. One Saturday morning there appeared
the following letter in the *Sentinel* :—

"SIR,—Last Sunday evening I happened to stray
into a chapel not a hundred miles from Water Lane.
Sir, it was a lovely evening and

> 'The glorious stars on high,
> Set like jewels in the sky,'

were circling their courses and, with the moon,
irresistibly reminded me of that blood which was
shed for the remission of sins. Sir, with my mind
attuned in that direction I entered the chapel. I
hoped to hear something of that Rock of Ages in
which, as the poet sings, we shall wish to hide
ourselves in years to come. But, sir, a young man,

evidently a young man occupied the pulpit, and great was my grief to find that the tainted flood of human philosophy had rolled through the town and was withering the truth as it is in Christ Jesus. Years ago that pulpit sent forth no uncertain sound, and the glorious gospel was proclaimed there—not a *German gospel*, sir—of our depravity and our salvation through Christ Jesus. Sir, I should like to know what the dear departed who endowed that chapel and are asleep in the Lord in that burying-ground, would say if they were to rise from their graves and sit in those pews again and hear what I heard—a sermon which might have been a week-day lecture. Sir, as I was passing through the town, I could not feel that I had done my duty without announcing to you the fact as above stated, and had not raised a humble warning from—Sir, yours truly, A CHRISTIAN TRAVELLER."

Notwithstanding the transparent artifice of the last paragraph, there was no doubt that the author of this precious production was Mr. Snale, and I at once determined to tax him with it. On the Monday morning I called on him, and found him in his shop.

"Mr. Snale," I said, "I have a word or two to say to you."

"Certainly, sir. What a lovely day it is! I hope you are very well, sir. Will you come upstairs."

But I declined to go upstairs, as it was probable I might meet Mrs. Snale there. So I said that we had better go into the counting-house, a little place boxed off at the end of the shop, but with no door to it. As soon as we got in I began.

"Mr. Snale, I have been much troubled by a letter which has appeared in last week's *Sentinel*. Although disguised it evidently refers to me, and to be perfectly candid with you, I cannot help thinking you wrote it."

"Dear me, sir, may I ask *why* you think so?"

"The internal evidence, Mr. Snale, is overwhelming; but if you did not write it, perhaps you will be good enough to say so."

Now Mr. Snale was a coward, but with a peculiarity which I have marked in animals of the rat tribe. He would double and evade as long as possible, but if he found there was no escape, he would turn and tear and fight to the last extremity.

"Mr. Rutherford, that is rather—ground of an, of an—what shall I say?—of an assumptive nature on which to make such an accusation, and I am not obliged to deny every charge which you may be pleased to make against me."

"Pardon me, Mr. Snale, do you then consider

what I have said is an accusation and a charge? Do you think that it was wrong to write such a letter?"

"Well, sir, I cannot exactly say that it was, but I must say, sir, that I do think it peculiar of you, peculiar of you, sir, to come here and attack one of your friends, who I am sure has always showed you so much kindness—to attack him, sir, with no proof."

Now Mr. Snale had not openly denied his authorship. But the use of the word "friend" was essentially a lie—just one of those lies which, by avoiding the form of a lie, have such a charm for a mind like his. I was roused to indignation.

"Mr. Snale, I will give you the proof which you want, and then you shall judge for yourself. The letter contains two lines of a hymn which you have misquoted. You made precisely that blunder in talking to the Sunday-school children on the Sunday before the letter appeared. You will remember that in accordance with my custom to visit the Sunday school occasionally, I was there on that Sunday afternoon."

"Well, sir, I've not denied I did write it."

"Denied you did write it!" I exclaimed, with gathering passion; "what do you mean by the subterfuge about your passing through the town and by your calling me your friend a minute ago? What would you have thought if anybody had written

anonymously to the *Sentinel*, and had accused you
of selling short measure? You would have said it
was a libel, and you would also have said that a
charge of that kind ought to be made publicly and
not anonymously. You seem to think, nevertheless,
that it is no sin to ruin me anonymously."

"Mr. Rutherford, I am sure I *am* your friend. I
wish you well, sir, both here"—and Mr. Snale tried
to be very solemn—"and in the world to come.
With regard to the letter, I don't see it as you do,
sir. But, sir, if you are going to talk in this tone, I
would advise you to be careful. We have heard, sir,"
—and here Mr. Snale began to simper and grin with
an indescribably loathsome grimace,—"that some
of your acquaintances in your native town are of
opinion that you have not behaved quite so well as you
should have done to a certain young lady of your
acquaintance; and what is more, we have marked
with pain here, sir, your familiarity with an atheist
and his daughter, and we have noticed their coming
to chapel, and we have also noticed a change in your
doctrine since these parties attended there."

At the word "daughter" Mr. Snale grinned
again, apparently to somebody behind me, and I
found that one of his shopwomen had entered the
counting-house, unobserved by me, while this conversation was going on, and that she was smirking

in reply to Mr. Snale's signals. In a moment the blood rushed to my brain. I was as little able to control myself as if I had been shot suddenly down a precipice.

" Mr. Snale, you are a contemptible scoundrel and a liar."

The effort on him was comical. He cried: " What, sir :—what do you mean, sir ?—a minister of the gospel—if you were not, I would—a liar—" and he swung round hastily on the stool on which he was sitting, to get off and grasp a yard measure which stood against the fireplace. But the stool slipped, and he came down ignominiously. I waited till he got up, but as he rose a carriage stopped at the door, and he recognised one of his best customers. Brushing the dust off his trousers, and smoothing his hair, he rushed out without his hat, and in a moment was standing obsequiously on the pavement bowing to his patron. I passed him in going out, but the oily film of subserviency on his face was not broken for an instant.

When I got home I bitterly regretted what had happened. I never regret anything more than the loss of self-mastery. I had been betrayed, and yet I could not for the life of me see how the betrayal could have been prevented. It was upon me so suddenly, that before a moment had been given me for reflection, the words were out of my mouth. I was distinctly conscious that the *I* had not said those words. They had been spoken by some other power working in me, which was beyond my reach. Nor could I foresee how to prevent such a fall for the future. The only advice, even now, which I can give to those who comprehend the bitter pangs of such self-degradation as passion brings, is to watch the first risings of the storm, and to say "Beware; be watchful," at the least indication of a tempest. Yet, after every precaution, we are at the mercy of the elements, and in an instant the sudden doubling of a cape may expose us, under a serene sky, to a blast which, taking us with all sails spread, may overset us and wreck us irretrievably.

My connection with the chapel was now obviously at an end. I had no mind to be dragged before a church meeting, and I determined to resign. After a little delay I wrote a letter to the deacons, explaining that I had felt a growing divergence from the theology taught heretofore in Water Lane, and I wished consequently to give up my connection with them. I received an answer stating that my resignation had been accepted; I preached a farewell sermon; and I found myself one Monday morning with a quarter's salary in my pocket, a few bills to pay, and a blank outlook. What was to be done? My first thought was towards Unitarianism, but when I came to cast up the sum total of what I was assured, it seemed so ridiculously small that I was afraid. The occupation of a merely miscellaneous lecturer had always seemed to me very poor. I could not get up Sunday after Sunday and retail to people little scraps suggested by what I might have been studying during the week; and with regard to the great subjects, for the exposition of which the Christian minister specially exists—how much did I know about them? The position of a minister who has a gospel to proclaim; who can go out and tell men what they are to do to be saved, was intelligible; but not so the position of a man who had no such gospel. What reason for continuance as a preacher could I claim? Why should people hear me rather than read books? I was alarmed to find, on making my reckoning, that the older I got the less I appeared to believe. Nakeder and nakeder had I become with the passage of every year, and I trembled to anticipate the complete emptiness to which before long I should be reduced. What the dogma of immortality was to me I have already described, and with regard to God I was no better. God was obviously not a person in the clouds, and what more was really firm under my feet than this —that the universe was governed by immutable laws? These laws were not what is commonly understood as God. Nor could I discern any ultimate tendency in them. Everything was full of contradiction. On the one hand was infinite misery; on the other there were exquisite adaptations producing the highest pleasure: on the one hand the mystery of a life-long disease, and on the other the equal mystery of the unspeakable glory of the sunrise on a summer's morning over a quiet summer sea. I happened to hear once an atheist discoursing on the follies of theism. If he had made the world, he would have made it much better. He would not have racked innocent souls with years of torture, that tyrants might live in splendour. He would not have permitted the earthquake to swallow up thousands of harmless mortals, and so forth. But, putting aside all dependence upon the theory of a coming rectification of such wrongs as these, the atheist's argument was shallow enough. It would have been easy to show that a world such as he imagines is unthinkable directly we are serious with our conception of it. On whatever lines the world may be framed, there must be *distinction*, *difference*, a higher and a lower; and the lower, relatively to the higher, must always be an evil. The *scale* upon which the higher and lower both are, makes no difference. The supremest bliss would

not be bliss if it were not *definable* bliss, that is to
say, in the sense that it has limits, marking it out
from something else not so supreme. Perfectly
uninterrupted infinite light, without shadow, is a
physical absurdity. I see a thing because it is
lighted, but also because of the differences of light,
or, in other words, because of shade, and without
shade the universe would be objectless, and in fact
invisible. The atheist was dreaming of shadowless
light, a contradiction in terms. Mankind may be
improved, and the improvement may be infinite,
and yet good and evil must exist. So with death
and life. Life without death is not life, and death
without life is equally impossible. But though all
this came to me, and was not only a great comfort
to me, but prevented any shallow prating like that
to which I listened from this lecturer, it could not
be said that it was a gospel from which to derive
apostolic authority. There remained morals. I
could become an instructor of morality. I could
warn tradesmen not to cheat, children to honour
their parents, and people generally not to lie. The
mission was noble, but I could not feel much
enthusiasm for it, and more than this, it was a fact
that reformations in morals have never been achieved
by mere directions to be good, but have always been
the result of an enthusiasm for some City of God,

or some supereminent person. Besides, the people
whom it was most necessary to reach would not be
the people who would, unsolicited, visit a Unitarian
meeting-house. As for a message of negations,
emancipating a number of persons from the dogma
of the Trinity or future punishment, and spending
my strength in merely demonstrating the nonsense of orthodoxy, my soul sickened at the very
thought of it. Wherein would men be helped, and
wherein should I be helped? There were only two
persons in the town who had ever been of any
service to me. One was Miss Arbour, and the other
was Mardon. But I shrank from Miss Arbour,
because I knew that my troubles had never been
hers. She belonged to a past generation, and as to
Mardon, I never saw him without being aware of
the difficulty of accepting any advice from him. He
was perfectly clear, perfectly secular, and was so
definitely shaped and settled, that his line of conduct
might always be predicted beforehand with certainty.
I knew very well what he thought about preaching,
and what he would tell me to do, or rather, what he
would tell me not to do. Nevertheless, after all, I
was a victim to that weakness which impels us to
seek the assistance of others when we know that
what they offer will be of no avail. Accordingly, I
called on him. Both he and Mary were at home,

and I was received with more than usual cordiality.
He knew already that I had resigned, for the news
was all over the town.   I said I was in great
perplexity.

"The perplexities of most persons arise," said
Mardon, "as yours probably arise, from not understanding exactly what you want to do.   For one
person who stumbles and falls with a perfectly
distinct object to be attained, I have known a score
whose disasters are to be attributed to their not
having made themselves certain what their aim is.
You do not know what you believe, consequently
you do not know how to act."

"What would you do if you were in my case?"

"Leave the whole business and prefer the meanest
handicraft.   You have no right to be preaching
anything doubtful.   You are aware what my creed
is.   I profess no belief in God, and no belief in what
hangs upon it.   Try and name, now, any earnest
conviction you possess, and see whether you have a
single one which I have not got."

"I *do* believe in God."

"There is nothing in that statement.   What do
you believe about Him?—that is the point.   You will
find that you believe nothing, in truth, which I do
not also believe of the laws which govern the universe
and man."

"I believe in an intellect of which these laws are the expression."

"Now what kind of an intellect can that be? You can assign to it no character in accordance with its acts. It is an intellect, if it be an intellect at all, which will swallow up a city, and will create the music of Mozart for me when I am weary; an intellect which brings to birth His Majesty King George IV., and the love of an affectionate mother for her child; an intellect which, in the person of a tender girl, shows an exquisite conscience, and in the person of one or two religious creatures whom I have known, shows a conscience almost inverted. I have always striven to prove to my theological friends that their mere affirmation of God is of no consequence. They may be affirming anything or nothing. The question, the all-important question is, *What* can be affirmed about Him?"

"Your side of the argument naturally admits of a more precise statement than mine. I cannot encompass God with a well-marked definition, but for all that, I believe in Him. I know all that may be urged against the belief, but I cannot help thinking that the man who looks upon the stars, or the articulation of a leaf, is irresistibly impelled, unless he has been corrupted by philosophy, to say, There is intellect there. It is the instinct of the child and of the man."

"I don't think so ; but grant it, and again I ask, *What* intellect is it ?"

"Again I say, I do not know."

"Then why dispute ? Why make such a fuss about it ?

"It really seems to me of immense importance whether you see this intellect or not, although you say it is of no importance. It appears to be of less importance than it really is, because I do not think that even you ever empty the universe of intellect. I believe that mind never worships anything but mind, and that you worship it when you admire the level bars of cloud over the setting sun. You think you eject mind, but you do not. I can only half imagine a belief which looks upon the world as a mindless blank, and if I could imagine it, it would be depressing in the last degree to me. I know that I have mind, and to live in a universe in which my mind is answered by no other would be unbearable. Better any sort of intelligence than none at all. But, as I have just said, your case admits of plainer statement than mine. You and I have talked this matter over before, and I have never gained a logical victory over you. Often I have felt thoroughly prostrated by you, and yet when I have left you the old superstition has arisen unsubdued. I do not know how it is, but I always feel that upon this, as upon many other subjects, I never can really speak myself. An unshapen thought presents itself to me, I look at it, and I do all in my power to give it body and expression, but I cannot. I am certain that there is something truer and deeper to be said about the existence of God than anything I have said, and what is more, I am certain of the presence of this something in me, but I cannot lift it to the light."

"Ah, you are now getting into the region of sentiment, and I am unable to accompany you. When my friends go into the cloud, I never try to follow them."

All this time Mary had been sitting in the armchair against the fireplace in her usual attitude, resting her head on her hand and with her feet crossed one over the other on the fender. She had been listening silently and motionless. She now closed her eyes and said—

"Father, father, it is not true."

"What is not true ?"

"I do not mean that what you have said about theology is not true, but you make Mr. Rutherford believe you are what you are not. Mr. Rutherford, father sometimes tells us he has no sentiment, but you must take no notice of him when he talks in that way. I always think of our visit to the seaside two years ago. The railway station was in a disagreeable part of the town, and when we came out we walked along a dismal row of very plain-looking houses. There were cards in the window with 'Lodgings' written on them, and father wanted to go in to ask the terms. I said that I did not wish to stay in such a dull street, but father could not afford to pay for a sea view, and so we went in to inquire. We then found that what we thought were the fronts of the houses were the backs, and that the fronts faced the bay. They had pretty gardens on the other side, and a glorious sunny prospect over the ocean."

Mardon laughed and said—

"Ah, Mary, there is no sea-front here, and no garden."

I took up my hat and said I must go. Both pressed me to stop, but I declined. Mardon urged me again, and at last said—

"I believe you've never once heard Mary sing."

Mary protested, and pleaded that as they had no piano, Mr. Rutherford would not care for her poor voice without any accompaniment. But I, too, protested that I should, and she got out the 'Messiah.' Her father took a tuning fork out of his pocket, and having struck it, Mary rose and began, 'He was despised.' Her voice was not powerful, but it was pure and clear, and she sang with that perfect taste which is begotten solely of a desire to honour the master. The song always had a profound charm for me. Partly this was due to association. The words and tones, which have been used to embody their emotions by those whom we have loved, are doubly expressive when we use them to embody our own. The song is potent too, because with utmost musical tenderness and strength, it reveals the secret of the influence of the story of Jesus. Nobody would be bold enough to cry, *That too is my case*, and yet the poorest and the humblest soul has a right to the consolation that Jesus was a man of sorrows and acquainted with grief. For some reason or the other, or for many reasons, Mary's voice wound itself into the very centre of my existence. I seemed to be listening to the tragedy of all human worth and genius. The ball rose in my throat, the tears mounted to my eyes, and I had to suppress myself rigidly. Presently she ceased. There was silence for a moment. I looked round, and saw that Mardon's face was on the table, buried in his hands. I felt that I had better go, for the presence of a stranger, when the heart is deeply stirred, is an intrusion. I noiselessly left the room, and Mary followed. When we got to the door she said : " I forgot that mother used to sing that song. I ought to have known better." Her own eyes were full; I thought the pressure of her hand as she bade me good-bye was a little firmer than usual, and as we parted an overmastering impulse seized me. I lifted her hand to my lips; without giving her time to withdraw it, I gave it one burning kiss, and passed out into the street. It was pouring with rain, and I had neither overcoat nor umbrella, but I heeded not the heavens, and not till I got home to my own fireless, dark, solitary lodgings, did I become aware of any contrast between the sphere into which I had been exalted and the earthly commonplace world by which I was surrounded.

CHAPTER VII.

EMANCIPATION.

THE old Presbyterian chapels throughout the country
have many of them become Unitarian, and occasionally, even in an agricultural village, a respectable red
brick building may be seen, dating from the time of
Queen Anne, in which a few descendants of the
eighteenth century heretics still testify against three
Gods in one and the deity of Jesus Christ. Generally
speaking, the attendance in these chapels is very
meagre, but they are often endowed, and so they are
kept open. There was one in the large straggling half-
village, half-town of D——, within about ten miles of
me, and the pulpit was then vacant. The income was
about £100 a year. The principal man there was a
small general dealer, who kept a shop in the middle
of the village street, and I had come to know him
slightly, because I had undertaken to give his boy a
few lessons to prepare him for admission to a boarding-school. The money in my pocket was coming to
an end, and as I did not suppose that any dishonesty

would be imposed on me, and although the prospect
was not cheering, I expressed my willingness to be
considered as a candidate. In the course of a week
or two I was therefore invited to preach. I was so
reduced that I was obliged to walk the whole distance
on the Sunday morning, and as I was asked to no
house, I went straight to the chapel, and loitered about
in the graveyard till a woman came and opened a
door at the back. I explained who I was, and sat
down in a Windsor chair against a small kitchen table
in the vestry. It was cold, but there was no fire, nor
were any preparations made for one. On the mantel-
shelf were a bottle of water and a glass, but as the
water had evidently been there for some time, it was
not very tempting. I waited in silence for about
twenty minutes, and my friend the dealer then came
in, and having shaken hands and remarked that it
was chilly, asked me for the hymns. These I gave him
and went into the pulpit. I found myself in a plain-
looking building designed to hold about two hundred people. There was a gallery opposite me, and the
floor was occupied with high, dark, brown pews, one
or two immediately on my right and left being surrounded with faded green curtains. I counted my
hearers, and discovered that there were exactly seventeen, including two very old labourers, who sat on a
form right at the end and near the door. The gallery

was quite empty, except a little organ or seraphine, I think it was called, which was played by a young woman. The dealer gave out the hymns, and accompanied the seraphine in a bass voice, singing the air. A weak whisper might be perceived from the rest of the congregation, but nothing more. I was somewhat taken aback at finding in the Bible a discourse which had been left by one of my predecessors. It was a funeral sermon, neatly written, and had evidently done duty on several occasions, although the allusions in it might be considered personal. The piety and good works of the departed were praised with emphasis, but the masculine pronouns originally used were altered above the lines all throughout to feminine pronouns, and the word "brother" to "sister," so that no difficulty might arise in reading it for either sex. I was faint, benumbed, and with no heart for anything. I talked for about half an hour about what I considered to be the real meaning of the death of Christ, thinking that this was a subject which might prove as attractive as any other. After the service the assembly of seventeen departed, save one thin elderly gentleman, who came into the vestry, and having made a slight bow, said: "Mr. Rutherford, will you come with me, if you please?" I accordingly followed him, almost in silence, through the village till we reached his house, where his wife, who had gone on before, received us. They had formerly kept the shop which the dealer now had, but had retired. They might both be about sixty-five, and were of about the same temperament, pale, thin, and ineffectual, as if they had been fed on gruel. We had dinner in a large room with an old-fashioned grate in it, in which was stuck a basket stove. I remember perfectly well what we had for dinner. There was a neck of mutton (cold), potatoes, cabbage, a suet pudding, and some of the strangest-looking ale I ever saw—about the colour of lemon juice, but what it was really like I do not know, as I did not drink beer. I was somewhat surprised at being asked whether I would take potatoes *or* cabbage, but thinking it was the custom of the country not to indulge in both at once, and remembering that I was on probation, I said "cabbage." Very little was spoken during dinner-time by anybody, and scarcely a word by my hostess. After dinner she cleared the things away, and did not again appear. My host drew near the basket stove, and having remarked that it was beginning to rain, fell into a slumber. At twenty minutes to two we sallied out for the afternoon service, and found the seventeen again in their places, excepting the two labourers, who were probably prevented by the wet from attending. The service was a repetition of that in the morning, and when I came down my host again came forward and presented me with nineteen shillings. The fee was a guinea, but from that two shillings were abated for my entertainment. He informed me at the same time that a farmer, who had been hearing me and who lived five miles on my road, would give me a lift. He was a very large, stout man, with a rosy countenance, which was somewhat of a relief after the gruel face of my former friend. We went round to a stable-yard, and I got into a four-wheeled chaise. His wife sat with him in front, and a biggish boy sat with me behind. When we came to the guide post which pointed down his lane, I got out, and was dismissed in the dark with the observation—uttered goodnaturedly and jovially, but not very help-fully—that he was " afraid I should have a wettish walk." The walk certainly was wettish, and as I had had nothing to eat or drink since my midday meal, I was miserable and desponding. But just before I reached home the clouds rolled off with the south-west wind into detached, fleecy masses, separated by liquid blue gulfs, in which were sowed the stars, and the effect upon me was what that sight, thank God, always has been—a sense of the infinite, extinguishing all mean cares.

I expected to hear no more from my Unitarian acquaintances, and was therefore greatly surprised when, a week after my visit, I received an invitation to " settle " amongst them. The usual month's trial

was thought unnecessary, as I was not altogether a
stranger to some of them.   I hardly knew what to
do.   I could not feel any enthusiasm at the prospect
of the engagement, but, on the other hand, there was
nothing else before me.   There is no more helpless
person in this world than a minister who is thrown
out of work.   At any rate, I should be doing no harm
if I went.   I pondered over the matter a good deal,
and then reflected that in a case where every opening is barred save one, it is our duty not to plunge
at an impassable barrier, but to take that one opening,
however unpromising it may be.   Accordingly I
accepted.   My income was to be a hundred a year,
and it was proposed that I should lodge with my
friend the retired dealer, who had the only two
rooms in the village which were available.   I went
to bid Mardon and Mary good-bye.   I had not seen
either of them since the night of the song.   To my
surprise I found them both away.   The blinds were
down and the door locked.   A neighbour, who heard
me knocking, came out and told me the news.
Mardon had had a dispute with his employer, and
had gone to London to look for work.   Mary had
gone to see a relative at some distance, and would
remain there until her father had determined what
was to be done.   I obtained the addresses of both of
them, and wrote to Mardon, telling him what my

destiny for the present was to be. To Mary I wrote
also, and to her I offered my heart. Looking back-
ward, I have sometimes wondered that I felt so little
hesitation; not that I have ever doubted since, that
what I did then was the one perfectly right thing
which I have done in my life, but because it was my
habit so to confuse myself with meditative indecision.
I had doubted before. I remember once being so
near engaging myself to a. girl that the desk was
open and the paper under my hand. But I held back,
could not make up my mind, and happily was stayed.
Had I not been restrained, I should for ever have
been miserable. The remembrance of this escape,
and the certain knowledge that of all beings whom
I knew I was most likely to be mistaken in an
emergency, always produced in me a torturing
tendency to inaction. There was no such tendency
now. I thought I chose Mary, but there was no
choice. The feeblest steel filing which is drawn to
a magnet, would think, if it had consciousness, that
it went to the magnet of its own free will. My
soul rushed to hers as if dragged by the force of a
loadstone. But she was not to be mine. I had a
note from her, a sweet note, thanking me with much
tenderness for my affectionate regard for her, but
saying that her mind had long since been made up.
She was an only child of a mother whom her father

had loved above everything in life, and she could never leave him nor suffer any affection to interfere with that which she felt for him and which he felt for her. I might well misinterpret him, and think it strange that he should be so much bound up in her. Few people knew him as she did.

The shock to me at first was overpowering, and I fell under the influence of that horrible monomania from which I had been free for so long. For weeks I was prostrate, with no power of resistance; the evil being intensified by my solitude. Of all the dreadful trials which human nature has the capacity to bear unshattered, the worst—as, indeed, I have already said—is the fang of some monomaniacal idea which cannot be wrenched out. A main part of the misery, as I have also said, lies in the belief that suffering of this kind is peculiar to ourselves. We are afraid to speak of it, and not knowing, therefore, how common it is, we are agonised with the fear lest it should be our own special disease. I managed to get through my duties, but how I cannot tell. Fortunately our calamities are not what they appear to be when they lie in perspective behind us or before us, for they actually consist of distinct moments, each of which is overcome by itself. I was helped by remembering my recovery before, and I was able now, as a reward of long-continued abstinence from wine, to lie much stiller, and wait with more patience till the cloud should lift. Mardon having gone to London, I was more alone than ever, but my love for Mary increased in intensity, and had a good deal to do with my restoration to health. It was a hopeless love, but to be in love hopelessly is more akin to sanity than careless, melancholy indifference to the world. I was relieved from myself by the anchorage of all my thoughts elsewhere. The pain of loss was great, but the main curse of my existence has not been pain or loss, but gloom; blind wandering in a world of black fog, haunted by apparitions. I am not going to expand upon the history of my silent relationship to Mary during that time. How can I? All that I felt has been described better by others; and if it had not been, I have no mind to attempt a description myself, which would answer no purpose. I continued to correspond with Mardon, but with Mary I interchanged no word. After her denial of me I should have dreaded the charge of selfishness if I had opened my lips again. I could not place myself in her affection before her father.

My work at the chapel was of the most lifeless kind. My people really consisted of five families—those of the retired dealer, the farmer who took me home the first day I preached, and a man who kept a shop in the village for the sale of all descriptions of goods, includ-

ing ready-made clothing and provisions. He had a
wife and one child. Then there was a superannuated
brassfounder, who had a large house near, and who
nominally was a Unitarian, having professed himself
a Unitarian in the town in which he was formerly
in business, where Unitarianism was flourishing. He
had come down here to cultivate, for amusement, a
few acres of ground, and play the squire at a cheap
rate. Released from active employment, he had
given himself over to eating and drinking, particularly the drinking of port wine. His wife was
dead, his sons were in business for themselves, and
his daughters all went to church. His connection
with the chapel was merely nominal, and I was very
glad it was so. I was hardly ever brought into
contact with him, except as trustee, and once I was
asked to his house to dinner; but the attempt to
make me feel my inferiority was so painful, and
the rudeness of his children was so marked, that I
never went again. There was also a schoolmaster,
who kept a low-priced boarding-school with a Unitarian connection. He lived, however, at such a
distance that his visits were very unfrequent. Sometimes on a fine summer's Sunday morning the boys
would walk over—about twenty of them altogether,
but this only happened perhaps half-a-dozen times
in the year. Although my congregation had a free-

thought lineage, I do not think that I ever had anything to do with a more petrified set. With one exception, they were meagre in the extreme. They were perfectly orthodox, except that they denied a few orthodox doctrines. Their method was as strict as that of the most rigid Calvinist. They plumed themselves, however, greatly on their intellectual superiority over the Wesleyans and Baptists round them; and so far as I could make out, the one topic they delighted in, was a demonstration of the unity of God from texts in the Bible, and a polemic against tri-theism. Sympathy with the great problems then beginning to agitate men, they had none. Socially they were cold, and the entertainment at their houses was pale and penurious. They never considered themselves bound to contribute a shilling to my support. There was an endowment of a hundred a year, and they were relieved from all further anxiety. They had no enthusiasm for their chapel, and came or stayed away on the Sunday just as it suited them, and without caring to assign any reason. The one exception was the wife of the shopkeeper. She was a contrast to her husband and all the rest. I do not think she was a Unitarian born and bred. She talked but little about theology, but she was devoted to her Bible, and had a fine sense for all the passages in it which had an experience in them. She was generous, spiritual, and possessed of an unswerving instinct for what was right. Oftentimes her prompt decisions were a scandal to her more sedate friends, who did not believe in any way of arriving at the truth except by rationalising, but she hardly ever failed to hit the mark. It was in questions of relationship between persons, of behaviour, and of morals, that her guidance was the surest. In such cases her force seemed to keep her straight, while the weakness of those around made it impossible for them not to wander, first on one side and then on the other. She was unflinching in her expressions, and at any sacrifice did her duty. It was her severity in obeying her conscience which not only gave authority to her admonitions, but was the source of her inspirations. She was not much of a reader, but she would read strange things. She had some old volumes of a magazine, a " Repository " of some kind—I have forgotten what, and she picked out from them some translations of German verses which she greatly admired. She was not a well-educated woman in the school sense of the word, and of several of our greatest names in literature had heard nothing. I do not think she knew anything about Shakespeare, and she never entered into the meaning of dramatic poetry. At all points her

path was her own, intersecting at every conceivable
angle the paths of her acquaintances, and never
straying along them, except just so far as they might
happen to be hers. While I was in the village an
event happened which caused much commotion.
Her son was serving in the shop, and there was in
the house at the time a nice-looking, clean servant
girl. Mrs. Lane, for that was my friend's name,
had meditated discharging her, for, with her usual
quickness, she thought she saw something in the
behaviour of her son to the girl which was peculiar.
One morning, however, both her son and the girl
were absent, and there was a letter upon the table
announcing that they were in a town about twenty
miles off and were married. The shock was great, and
a tumult of voices arose, confusing counsel. Mrs.
Lane said but little, but never wavered an instant.
Leaving her husband to "consider what was best to
be done," she got out the gig, drove herself over to
her son's lodging, and presented herself to her amazed
daughter-in-law, who fell upon her knees and prayed
for pity. "My dear," said Mrs. Lane, "get up this
instant; you are my daughter. Not another word.
I've come to see what you want." And she kissed
her tenderly. The girl was at heart a good girl.
She was so bound to her late mistress and her new
mother by this behaviour, that the very depths in

her opened, and she loved Mrs. Lane ever after with
almost religious fervour. She was taught a little up
to her son's level, and a happier marriage I never
knew. Mrs. Lane told me what she had done, but
she had no theory about it. She merely said that
she knew it to be the right thing to do. She was
very fond of getting up early in the morning and
going out, and in such a village this was an eccen-
tricity bordering almost on lunacy. At five o'clock
she would often be wandering about in her large
garden. She was a great lover of order in the house,
and kept it well under control, but I do not think I
ever surprised her when she was so busy that she
would not easily, and without any apparent sacrifice,
leave what she was doing to come and talk with me.
As I have said, the world of books in which I lived
was almost altogether shut to her, but yet she was
the only person in the village whose conversation
was lifted out of the petty and personal into the
region of the universal. I have been thus particular
in describing her—I fear without raising any image
of her—because she was of incalculable service to
me. I languished from lack of life, and her mere
presence, so exuberant in its full vivacity, was like
mountain air. Furthermore, she was not troubled
much with my philosophical difficulties. They had
not come in her path. Her world was the world of

men and women—more particularly of those she knew, and it was a world in which it did me good to dwell. She was all the more important to me, because outside our own little circle there was no society whatever. The Church and the other dissenting bodies considered us as non-Christian. I often wondered that Mr. Lane retained his business, and, indeed, he would have lost it if he had not established a reputation for honesty, which drew customers to him, who, notwithstanding the denunciations of the parson, preferred tea with some taste in it from a Unitarian to the insipid wood-flavoured stuff which was sold by the grocer who believed in the Trinity.

CHAPTER VIII.

PROGRESS IN EMANCIPATION.

I WAS with my Unitarian congregation for about a twelvemonth. My life during that time, save so far as my intercourse with Mrs. Lane, and one other friend presently to be mentioned, was concerned, was as sunless and joyless as it had ever been. Imagine me living by myself, roaming about the fields, and absorbed mostly upon insoluble problems with which I never made any progress, and which tended to draw me away from what enjoyment of life there was which I might have had. One day I was walking along under the south side of a hill, which was a great place for butterflies, and I saw a man, apparently about fifty years old, coming along with a butterfly net. He did not see me, for he looked about for a convenient piece of turf, and presently sat down, taking out a sandwich box, from which he produced his lunch. His occupation did not particularly attract me, but in those days, if I encountered a new person who was not repulsive, I

was always as eager to make his acquaintance as
if he perchance might solve a secret for me, the
answer to which I burned to know. I have been
disappointed now so many times, and have found
that nobody has much more to tell me, that my
curiosity has somewhat abated, but even now, the
news that anybody who has the reputation for
intelligence has come near me, makes me restless to
see him. I accordingly saluted the butterfly catcher,
who returned the salutation kindly, and we began to
talk. He told me that he had come seven miles
that morning to that spot, because he knew that it
was haunted by one particular species of butterfly
which he wished to get; and as it was a still, bright
day, he hoped to find a specimen. He had been
unsuccessful for some years. Presupposing that I
knew all about his science, he began to discourse
upon it with great freedom, and he ended by saying
that he would be happy to show me his collection,
which was one of the finest in the country.

"But I forget," said he, "as I always forget in
such cases, perhaps you don't care for butterflies."

"I take much interest in them. I admire exceedingly the beauty of their colours."

"Ah, yes, but you don't care for them scientifi-
cally, or for collecting them."

"No, not particularly. I cannot say I ever

saw much pleasure in the mere classification of insects." .

"Perhaps you are devoted to some other science?"

"No, I am not."

"Well, I daresay it looks absurd for a man at my years to be running after a moth. I used to think it was absurd, but I am wiser now. However, I cannot stop to talk ; I shall lose the sunshine. The first time you are anywhere near me, come and have a look. You will alter your opinion."

Some weeks afterwards I happened to be in the neighbourhood of the butterfly catcher's house, and I called. He was at home, and welcomed me cordially. The first thing he did was to show me his little museum. It was really a wonderful exhibition, and as I saw the creatures in lines, and noted the amazing variations of the single type, I was filled with astonishment. Seeing the butterflies systemati-cally arranged was a totally different thing to seeing a butterfly here and there, and gave rise to altogether new thoughts. My friend knew his subject from end to end, and I envied him his mastery of it. I had often craved the mastery of some one particular pro-vince, be it ever so minute. I half or a quarter knew a multitude of things, but no one thing thoroughly, and was never sure, just when I most wanted to be sure. We got into conversation, and I was urged to stay to dinner. I consented, and found that my friend's household consisted of himself alone. After dinner, as we became a little more communicative, I asked him when and how he took to this pursuit.

"It will be twenty-six years ago next Christmas," said he, "since I suffered a great calamity. You will forgive my saying anything about it, as I have no assurance that the wound which looks healed may not break out again. Suffice to say, that for some ten years or more my thoughts were almost entirely occupied with death and our future state. There is a strange fascination about these topics to many people, because they are topics which permit a great deal of dreaming, but very little thinking: in fact, true thinking, in the proper sense of the word, is impossible in dealing with them. There is no rigorous advance from one position to another, which is really all that makes thinking worth the name. Every man can imagine or say cloudy things about death and the future, and feel himself here, at least, on a level with the ablest brain which he knows. I went on gazing gloomily into dark emptiness, till all life became nothing for me. I did not care to live, because there was no assurance of existence beyond. By the strangest of processes, I neglected the world, because I had so short a time to be in it. It is with absolute horror now that I look back upon those

days, when I lay as if alive in a coffin of lead. All
passions and pursuits were nullified by the ever-
abiding sense of mortality. For years this mood
endured, and I was near being brought down to the
very dust. At last, by the greatest piece of good
fortune, I was obliged to go abroad. The change,
and the obligation to occupy myself about many
affairs, was an incalculable blessing to me. While
travelling I was struck with the remarkable and
tropical beauty of the insects, and especially of the
butterflies. I captured a few, and brought them
home. On showing them to a friend, learned in
such matters, I discovered that they were rare, and
I had a little cabinet made for them. I looked into
the books, found what it was which I had got, and
what I had not got. Next year it was my duty to
go abroad again, and I went with some feeling akin to
pleasure, for I wished to add to my store. I increased
it considerably, and by the time I returned I had as
fine a show as any private person might wish to
possess. A good deal of my satisfaction, perhaps,
was unaccountable, and no rational explanation can
be given of it. But men should not be too curious in
analysing and condemning any means which nature
devises to save them from themselves, whether it be
coins, old books, curiosities, butterflies, or fossils.
And yet my newly-acquired passion was not alto-

gether inexplicable. I was the owner of something
which other persons did not own, and in a little
while, in my own limited domain I was supreme.
No man either can study any particular science
thoroughly without transcending it; and it is an
utter mistake to suppose, that because a student
sticks to any one branch, he necessarily becomes
contracted. However, I am not going to philo-
sophise; I do not like it. All I can say is, that I
shun all those metaphysical speculations of former
years as I would a path which leads to madness.
Other people may be able to occupy themselves
with them and be happy; I cannot. I find quite
enough in my butterflies to exercise my wonder,
and yet, on the other hand, my study is not a mere
vacant, profitless stare. When you saw me that
morning, I was trying to obtain an example which
I have long wanted to fill up a gap. I have looked
for it for years, but have missed it. But I know
it has been seen lately where we met, and I shall
triumph at last."

A good deal of all this was to me incomprehensible. It seemed mere solemn trifling compared with
the investigation of those great questions with which
I had been occupied, but I could not resist the con-
tagion of my friend's enthusiasm when he took me
to his little library, and identified his treasures with

pride, pointing out at the same time those in which he was deficient. He was specially exultant over one minute creature which he had caught himself, which he had not as yet seen figured, and he proposed going to the British Museum almost on purpose to see if he could find it there.

When I got home I made inquiries into the history of my entomologist. I found that years ago he had married a delicate girl, of whom he was devotedly fond. She died in childbirth, leaving him completely broken. Her offspring, a boy, survived, but he was a cripple, and grew up deformed. As he neared manhood he developed a satyr-like lustfulness, which was almost uncontrollable, and made it difficult to keep him at home without constraint. He seemed to have no natural affection for his father, nor for anybody else, but was cunning with the base beastly cunning of the ape. The father's horror was infinite. This thing was his only child, and the child of the woman whom he worshipped. He was excluded from all intercourse with friends; for, as the boy could not be said to be mad, he could not be shut up. After years of inconceivable misery, however, lust did deepen into absolute lunacy, and the crooked, misshapen monster was carried off to an asylum, where he died, and the father well-nigh went there too.

Before I had been six months amongst the Unitarians, I found life even more intolerable with them than it had been with the Independents. The difference of a little less belief was nothing. The question of Unitarianism was altogether dead to me; and although there was a phase of the doctrine of God's unity which would now and then give me an opportunity for a few words which I felt, it was not a phase for which my hearers in the least cared or which they understood. Here, as amongst the Independents, there was the same lack of personal affection, or even of a capability of it—excepting always Mrs. Lane—and, in fact, it was more distressing amongst the Unitarians than amongst the orthodox. The desire for something like sympathy and love absolutely devoured me. I dwelt on all the instances in poetry and history in which one human being had been bound to another human being, and I reflected that my existence was of no earthly importance to anybody. I could not altogether lay the blame on myself. God knows that I would have stood against a wall and have been shot for any man or woman whom I loved, as cheerfully as I would have gone to bed, but nobody seemed to wish for such a love, or to know what to do with it. Oh the humiliations under which this weakness has bent me! Often and often I have thought that I have discovered some-

body who would really comprehend the value of a
passion which would tell everything and venture
everything. I have overstepped all bounds of
etiquette in obtruding myself on him, and have
opened my heart even to shame. I have then
found that it was all on my side; that for every
dozen times I went to his house, he would come
to mine once, and only when pressed: I have
languished in sickness for a month without his
finding it out; and I have become assured that if I
were to drop into the grave, he would get up the next
morning after hearing the news and perhaps never
give me a thought during the day. If I had been
born a hundred years earlier, I should have transferred this burning longing to the unseen God and
have become a devotee. But I was a hundred years
too late, and I felt that it was mere cheating of
myself and a mockery to think about love for the
only God whom I knew, the forces which maintained
the universe. I am now getting old, and have altered
in many things. The hunger and thirst of those
years have abated, or rather, the fire has had ashes
heaped on it, so that it is well-nigh extinguished.
I have been repulsed into self-reliance and reserve,
having learned wisdom by experience; but still I
know that the desire has not died, as so many other
desires have died, by the natural evolution of age.

It has been forcibly suppressed, and that is all. If anybody who reads these words of mine should be offered by any young dreamer such a devotion as I once had to offer, and had to take back again refused so often, let him in the name of all that is sacred accept it. It is simply the most precious thing in existence. Had I found anybody who would have thought so, my life would have been redeemed into something which I have often imagined, but now shall never know.

I determined to leave, but what to do I could not tell. I was fit for nothing, and yet I could not make up my mind to accept a life which was simply living. It must be a life through which some benefit was conferred upon my fellow-creatures. This was mainly delusion. I had not then learned to correct this natural instinct to be of some service to mankind by the thought of the boundlessness of infinity and of nature's profuseness. I had not come to reflect that, taking into account her eternities, and absolute exhaustlessness, it was folly in me to fret and fume, and I therefore clung to the hope that I might employ myself in some way which, however feebly, would help mankind a little to the realisation of an ideal. But I was not the man for such a mission. I lacked altogether that concentration which binds up the scattered powers into one resistless energy, and I lacked faith. All I could do was to play the vagrant in literature, picking up here and there an idea which attracted me, and presenting it to my flock on the Sunday; the net result being next to nothing. However, existence like that which I had been leading was intolerable, and change it I must. I accordingly resigned, and with ten pounds in my pocket, which was all that remained after paying my bills, I came to London, thinking that until I could settle what to do, I would try and teach in a school. I called on an agent somewhere near the Strand, and after a little negotiation, was engaged by a gentleman who kept a private establishment at Stoke Newington. Thither I accordingly went one Monday afternoon in January, about two days before the term commenced. When I got there, I was shown into a long schoolroom, which had been built out from the main building. It was dark, save for one candle, and was warmed by a stove. The walls were partly covered with maps, and at one end of the room hung a diagram representing a globe, on which an immense amount of wasted ingenuity had been spent to produce the illusion of solidity. The master, I was told, was out, and in this room with one candle I remained till nine o'clock. At that time a servant brought me some bread and cheese on a small tray, with half-a-

pint of beer. I asked for water, which was given
me, and she then retired. The tray was set down on
the master's raised desk, and sitting there I ate my
supper in silence, looking down upon the dimly-
lighted forms, and forward into the almost absolute
gloom. At ten o'clock a man, who seemed as if he
were the knife and boot cleaner, came and said he
would show me where I was to sleep. We passed
through the schoolroom into a kind of court, where
there was a ladder standing against a trap-door.
He told me that my bedroom was up there, and that
when I got up I could leave the ladder down, or
pull it up after me, just as I pleased. I ascended
and found a little chamber, duly furnished with a
chest of drawers, bed, and washhand stand. It was
tolerably clean and decent; but who shall describe
what I felt. I went to the window and looked out.
There were scattered lights here and there marking
roads, but as they crossed one another, and now and
then stopped where building had ceased, the effect
they produced was that of bewilderment with no
clue to it. Further off was the great light of London,
like some unnatural dawn, or the illumination from
a fire which could not itself be seen. I was overcome with the most dreadful sense of loneliness. I
suppose it is the very essence of passion, using the
word in its literal sense, that no account can be

given of it by the reason. Reflecting on what I suffered then, I cannot find any solid ground for it, and yet there are not half-a-dozen days or nights of my life which remain with me like that one. I was beside myself with a kind of terror, which I cannot further explain. It is possible for another person to understand grief for the death of a friend, bodily suffering, or any emotion which has a distinct cause, but how shall he understand the most horrible of all calamities, the nameless dread, the efflux of all vitality, the ghostly haunting horror which is so nearly akin to madness? It is many years ago since that evening, but while I write I am at the window still, and the yellow flare of the city is still in my eyes. I remember the thought of all the happy homes which lay around me, in which dwelt men who had found a position, an occupation, and, above all things, affection. I know the cause-lessness of a good deal of all those panic fears, and all that suffering, and I tremble to think how thin is the floor on which we stand which separates us from the bottomless abyss.

The next morning I went down into the school-room, and after I had been there for some little time, the proprietor of the school made his appearance. He was not a bad man, nor even unkind in his way, but he was utterly uninteresting, and as common-

K

place as might be expected after having for many
years done nothing but fight a very uphill battle
in boarding the sons of tradesfolk, and teaching
them, at very moderate rates, the elements of Latin,
and the various branches of learning which consti-
tute what is called a commercial education.   He
said that he expected some of the boys back that
day ; that when they came, he should wish me to
take my meals with them, but that meanwhile he
would be glad if I would breakfast with him and his
wife.   This accordingly I did.   What his wife was
like I have almost entirely forgotten, and I only saw
her once again.   After breakfast he said I could go
for a walk, and for a walk I went ; wandering about
the dreary intermingled chaos of fields with damaged
hedges, and new roads divided into building plots.

Meanwhile one or two of the boys had made their
appearance, and I therefore had my dinner with
them.   After dinner, as there was nothing particular
to do, I was again dismissed with them for a walk
just as the light of the winter afternoon was fading.
My companions were dejected, and so was I.   The
wind was south-easterly, cold and raw, and the smoke
came up from the region about the river and shrouded
all the building plots in fog.   I was now something
more than depressed.   It was absolutely impossible
to endure such a state of things any longer, and I

determined that, come what might, I would not stop.
I considered whether I should leave without saying
a word, that is to say, whether I should escape, but
I feared pursuit and some unknown legal proceedings.
When I got home, therefore, I sought the principal,
and informed him that I felt so unwell that I was
afraid I must throw up my engagement at once. He
naturally observed that this was a serious business for him; that my decision was very hasty—
what was the matter with me? I might get better;
but concluded, after my reiterated asseverations that
I must go, with a permission to resign, only on one
condition, that I should obtain an equally efficient
substitute at the same salary. I was more agitated
than ever. With my natural tendency to believe the
worst, I had not the least expectation of finding anybody who would release me. The next morning I
departed on my errand. I knew a poor student who
had been at college with me, and who had nothing
to do, and to him I betook myself. I strove—as even
now I firmly believe—not to make the situation seem
any better than it was, and he consented to take
it. I have no clear recollection of anything that
happened till the following day, excepting that I
remember with all the vividness of actual and
present sensuous perception, lugging my box down
the ladder and sending for a cab. I was in a fever lest

anything should arrest me, but the cab came, and I departed. When I had got fairly clear of the gates, I literally cried tears of joy—the first and the last of my life. I am constrained now, however, to admit that my trouble was but a bubble blown of air, and I doubt whether I have done any good by dwelling upon it.

CHAPTER VIII.

OXFORD STREET.

UNTIL I had actually left, I hardly knew where I was going, but at last I made up my mind I would go to Reuben Shapcott, another fellow-student, whom I knew to be living in lodgings in one of the streets just then beginning to creep over the unoccupied ground between Camden Town and Haverstock Hill, near the Chalk Farm turnpike gate. To his address I betook myself, and found him not at home. He, like me, had been unsuccessful as a minister, and wrote a London letter for two country papers, making up about £100 or £120 a year by preaching occasionally in small Unitarian chapels in the country. I waited till his return, and told him my story. He advised me to take a bed in the house where he was staying, and to consider what could be done. At first I thought I would consult Mardon, but I could not bring myself to go near him. How was I to behave in Mary's presence? During the last few months she had been so continually before me, that it would have been absolutely impossible for me to treat her with assumed indifference. I could not have trusted myself to attempt it. When I had been lying alone and awake at night, I had thought of all the endless miles of hill and valley that lay outside my window, separating me from the one house in which I could be at peace; and at times I scarcely prevented myself from getting up and taking the mail train and presenting myself at Mardon's door, braving all consequences. With the morning light, however, would come cooler thoughts, and a dull sense of impossibility. This, I know, was not pure love for her; it was a selfish passion for relief. But then I have never known what is meant by a perfectly pure love. When Christian was in the Valley of the Shadow of Death, and being brought to the mouth of hell, was forced to put up his sword and could do no other than cry, *O Lord, I beseech Thee, deliver my soul*, he heard a voice going before him and saying, *Though I walk through the Valley of the Shadow of Death, I will fear none ill, for Thou art with me.* And by and by the day broke." "Then," said Christian, "He hath turned the Shadow of Death into morning. Whereupon Christian sang—

> "Oh world of wonders! (I can say no less)
> That I should be preserved in that distress
> That I have met with here! Oh, blessed be
> That hand that from it hath delivered me!"

This was Christian's love for God, and for God as his helper. Was that perfectly pure? However, this is a digression. I determined to help myself in my own way, and thought I would try the publishers. One morning I walked from Camden Town to Paternoster Row. I went straightway into two or three shops and asked whether they wanted anybody. I was ready to do the ordinary work of a publisher's assistant, and aspired no higher. I met with several refusals, some of them not over polite, and the degradation—for so I felt it—of wandering through the streets and suing for employment cut me keenly. I remember one man in particular, who spoke to me with the mechanical brutality with which probably he replied to a score of similar applications every week. He sat in a little glass box at the end of a long dark room lighted with gas. It was a bitterly cold room, with no contrivance for warming it, but in his box there was a fire burning for his own special benefit. He surveyed all his clerks unceasingly, and woe betide the unhappy wretch who was caught idling. He and his slaves reminded me of the thrashing machine which is worked by horses walking round in a ring, the driver being perched on a high stool in the middle and armed with a long whip. While I was waiting his pleasure, he came out and spoke to one or two of his miserable subordinates words of directest and sharpest rebuke, without anger or the least loss of self-possession, and yet without the least attempt to mitigate their severity. I meditated much upon him. If ever I had occasion to rebuke anybody, I always did it apologetically, unless I happened to be in a flaming passion—and this was my habit, not from any respectable motive of consideration for the person rebuked, but partly because I am timid, and partly because I shrink from giving pain. This man said with perfect ease what I could not have said unless I had been wrought up to white heat. With all my dislike to him, I envied him: I envied his complete certainty; for although his language was harsh in the extreme, he was always sure of his ground, and the victim upon whom his lash descended could never say that he had given absolutely no reason for the chastisement, and that it was altogether a mistake. I envied also his ability to make himself disagreeable and care nothing about it; his power to walk in his own path, and his resolve to succeed, no matter what the cost might be. As I left him, it occurred to me that I might be more successful perhaps with a publisher of whom I had heard, who published and sold books of a sceptical turn. To him I accordingly went, and although I had no introductions or recommendatory letters, I was received, if not with a cordiality, at least with an interest which surprised me. He took me into a little back shop, and after hearing patiently what I wanted, he asked me somewhat abruptly what I thought of the miracles in the Bible. This was a curious question if he wished to understand my character; but his mind so constantly revolved in one circle, and existed so completely by hostility to the prevailing orthodoxy, that belief or disbelief in it was the standard by which he judged men. It was a very absurd standard doubtless, but no more absurd than many others, and not so absurd then as it would be now, when heresy is becoming more fashionable. I explained to him as well as I could what my position was; that I did not suppose that the miracles actually happened as they are recorded, but that, generally speaking, the miracle was a very intense statement of a divine truth; in fact, a truth which was felt with a more than common intensity seemed to take naturally a miraculous expression. Hence, so far from neglecting the miraculous stories of the Bible as simply outside me, I rejoiced in them, more, perhaps, than in the plain historical or didactic prose. He seemed content, although hardly to comprehend, and the result was that he asked me if I would help him in his business. In order to do this, it would be more economical if I would live in his house, which was too big for him. He promised to give me £40 a year, in addition to board and lodging. I joyously assented, and the bargain was struck. The next day I came to my new quarters. I found that he was a bachelor, with a niece, apparently about four or five and twenty years old, acting as a housekeeper, who assisted him in literary work. My own room was at the top of the house, warm, quiet, and comfortable, although the view was nothing but a wide reaching assemblage of chimney pots. My hours were long—from nine in the morning till seven in the evening; but this I did not mind. I felt that if I was not happy, I was at least protected, and that I was with a man who cared for me, and for whom I cared. The first day I went there, he said that I could have a fire in my bedroom whenever I chose, so that I could always retreat to it when I wished to be by myself. As for my duties, I was to sell his books, keep his accounts, read proofs, run errands, and, in short, do just what he did himself. After my first morning's work we went upstairs to dinner, and I was introduced to "my niece Theresa." I was rather surprised that I should have been admitted to a house in which there lived a young woman with no mother nor aunt, but this surprise ceased when I came to know more of Theresa and her uncle. She had yellowish hair which was naturally waved, a big arched head, greyish blue eyes, so far as I could make out, and a mouth which, although it had curves in it, was compressed and indicative of great force of character. She was rather short, with square shoulders, and she had a singularly vigorous firm walk. She had a way, when she was not eating or drinking, of sitting back in her chair at table and looking straight at the person with whom she was talking. Her uncle, whom, by the way, I had forgotten to name—his name was Wollaston—happened to know some popular preacher whom I knew, and I said that I wondered so many people went to hear him, for I believed him to be a hypocrite, and hypocrisy was one of the easiest of crimes to discover. Theresa, who had hitherto been silent, and was reclining in her usual attitude, instantly broke out with an emphasis and directness which quite startled me.

"The easiest to discover, do you think, Mr. Rutherford; I think it is the most difficult, at least for ordinary persons; and when they do discover it, I believe they like it, especially if it is successful. They like the sanction it gives to their own hypocrisy. They like a man to come to them who will say to them, 'We are all hypocrites together,' and who will put his finger to his nose and comfort them. Don't you think so yourself?"

In conversation I was always a bad hand at assuming a position contrary to the one assumed by the person to whom I might be talking; nor could I persistently maintain my own position if it happened to be opposed. I always rather tried to see as my opponent saw, and to discover how much there was in him with which I could sympathise. I therefore assented weakly to Theresa, and she seemed disappointed. Dinner was just over; she got up and rang the bell and went out of the room.

I found my work very hard, and some of it even loathsome. Particularly loathsome was that part of it which brought me into contact with the trade. I had to sell books to the booksellers' assistants, and I had to collect books myself. These duties are usually undertaken in large establishments by men specially trained, who receive a low rate of wages, and who are rather a rough set. It was totally different work to anything I had ever had to do before, and I suffered as a man with soft hands would suffer, who was suddenly called to be a blacksmith or a dock-labourer. Specially, too, did I miss the country. London lay round me like a mausoleum. I got into the habit of rising very early in the morning and walking out to Kensington Gardens and back before breakfast, varying my route occasionally so as even to reach Battersea Bridge, which was always a favourite spot with me. Kensington Gardens and Battersea Bridge were poor substitutes for the downs, and for the level stretch by the river towards the sea where I first saw Mardon, but we make too much of circumstances, and the very pressure of London produced a sensibility to whatever loveliness could be apprehended there, which was absent when loveliness was always around me. The stars seen in Oxford Street late one night; a sunset one summer evening from Lambeth pier; and above everything, Piccadilly very early one summer morning, abide with me still, when much that was more romantic has been forgotten. On the whole, I was not unhappy. The constant outward occupation prevented any eating of the heart or undue brooding over problems which were insoluble, at least for my intellect, and on that very account fascinated me the more. I do not think that Wollaston cared much for me personally. He was a curious compound, materialistic yet impulsive, and for ever drawn to some new thing; without any love for anybody particularly, as far as I could see, and yet with much more general kindness and philanthropy than many a man possessing much stronger sympathies and antipathies. There was no holy of holies in him, into which one or two of the elect could occasionally be admitted and feel God to

be there. He was no temple, but rather a comfortable hospitable house open to all friends, well
furnished with books and pictures, and free to every
guest from garret to cellar. He had "liberal"
notions about the relationship between the sexes.
Not that he was a libertine, but he disbelieved in
marriage, excepting for so long as husband and wife
are a necessity to one another. If one should find
the other uninteresting, or somebody else more
interesting, he thought there ought to be a separation. All this I soon learned from him, for he was
communicative without any reserve. His treatment
of his niece was peculiar. He would talk on all
kinds of subjects before her, for he had a theory that
she ought to receive precisely the same social training as men, and should know just what men knew.
He was never coarse, but on the other hand he would
say things to her in my presence, which would bring
a flame into my face. What the evil consequences
of this might be, I could not at once foresee, but one
good result obviously was, that in his house there
was nothing of that execrable practice of talking
down to women; there was no change of level when
women were present. One day he began to speak
about a novel which everybody was reading then,
and I happened to say that I wished people who
wrote novels would not write as if love were the

very centre and sum of human existence. A man's life was made up of so much besides love, and yet novelists were never weary of repeating the same story, telling it over and over again in a hundred different forms.

"I do not agree with you," said Theresa. "I disagree with you utterly. I dislike foolish inane sentiment—it makes me sick ; but I do believe, in the first place, that no man was ever good for anything who has not been devoured, I was going to say, by a great devotion to a woman. The lives of your great men are as much the history of women whom they adored as of themselves. Dante, Byron, Shelley, it is the same with all of them, and there is no mistake about it; it is the great fact of life. What would Shakespeare be without it? and Shakespeare *is* life. A man, worthy to be named a man, will find the fact of love perpetually confronting him till he reaches old age, and if he be not ruined by worldliness or dissipation, will be troubled by it when he is fifty as much as he was when he was twenty-five. It is the subject of all subjects. People abuse love, and think it the cause of half the mischief in the world. It is the one thing that keeps the world straight, and if it were not for that overpowering instinct, human nature would fall asunder; would be the prey of inconceivable selfishnesses and vices, and finally, there would be universal suicide. I did not intend to be eloquent. I hate being eloquent. But you did not mean what you said; you spoke from the head or teeth merely."

Theresa's little speech was delivered not with any heat of the blood. There was no excitement in her grey eyes, nor did her cheek burn. Her brain seemed to rule everything. This was an idea she had, and she kindled over it because it was an idea. It was impossible, of course, that she should say what she did without some movement of the organ in her breast, but how much share this organ had in her utterances, I never could make out. How much was due to the interest which she as a looker-on felt in men and women, and how much was due to herself as a woman, was always a mystery to me. She was fond of music, and occasionally I would ask her to play to me. She had a great contempt for bungling, and not being a professional player, she never would try a piece in my presence of which she was not perfectly master. She particularly liked to play Mozart, and on my asking her once to play a piece of Beethoven, she turned round upon me and said : "You like Beethoven best. I knew you would. He encourages a luxurious revelling in the incomprehensible and indefinably sublime. He is not good for you."

My work was so hard, and the hours were so long, that I had little or no time for reading, nor for thinking either, except so far as Wollaston and Theresa made me think. Wollaston himself took rather to science, although he was not scientific, and made a good deal of what he called psychology. He was not very profound, but he had picked up a few phrases, or if this word is too harsh, a few ideas about metaphysical matters from authors who contemned metaphysics, and with these he was perfectly satisfied. A stranger listening to him would at first consider him well read, but would soon be undeceived, and would find that these ideas were acquired long ago; that he had never gone behind or below them, and that they had never fructified in him, but were like hard stones, which he rattled in his pocket. He was totally unlike Mardon. Mardon, although he would have agreed with many of Wollaston's results, differed entirely from him in the processes by which they had been brought about; and a mental comparison of the two often told me what I had been told over and over again, that what we believe is not of so much importance as the path by which we travel to it. Theresa too, like her uncle, eschewed metaphysics, but she was a woman, and a woman's impulses supplied in her the lack of those deeper questionings, and at times prompted them. She was far more

L

original than he was, and was impatient of the
narrowness of the circle in which he moved. Her
love of music, for example, was a thing incomprehensible to him, and I do not remember that he ever sat
for a quarter of an hour really listening to it. He
would read the newspaper or do anything while she
was playing. She never resented his inattention,
except when he made a noise, and then, without any
rebuke, she would break off and go away. This
mode of treatment was the outcome of one of her
theories. She disbelieved altogether in punishment,
except when it was likely to do good, either to the
person punished or to others. "A good deal of
punishment," she used to say, " is mere useless pain."

Both Theresa and her uncle were kind and human,
and I endeavoured to my utmost to repay them by
working my hardest. My few hours of leisure were
sweet, and when I spent them with Wollaston and
Theresa, were interesting. I often asked myself
why I found this mode of existence more tolerable
than any other I had hitherto enjoyed. I had, it
is true, an hour or two's unspeakable peace in the
early morning, but, as I have said, at nine my toil
commenced, and, with a very brief interval for
meals, lasted till seven. After seven I was too
tired to do anything by myself, and could only
keep awake if I happened to be in company. One

reason certainly why I was content, was Theresa herself. She was a constant study to me, and I could not for a long time obtain any consistent idea of her. She was not a this or a that or the other. She could not be summarily dismissed into any ordinary classification. At first I was sure she was hard, but I found by the merest accident that nearly all her earnings were given with utmost secrecy to support a couple of poor relatives. Then I thought her self-conscious, but this, when I came to think upon it, seemed a mere word. She was one of those women, and very rare they are, who deal in ideas, and reflectiveness must be self-conscious. At times she appeared passionless, so completely did her intellect dominate, and so superior was she to all the little arts and weaknesses of women ; but this was a criticism she contradicted continually. There was very little society at the Wollastons', but occasionally a few friends called. One evening there was a little party, and the conversation flagged. Theresa said that it was a great mistake to bring people together with nothing special to do but talk. Nothing is more tedious than to be in a company assembled for no particular reason, and every host, if he asks more than two persons at the outside, ought to provide some entertainment. Talking is worth nothing unless it is perfectly spontaneous, and

it cannot be spontaneous if there are sudden and
blank silences, and nobody can think of a fresh
departure. The master of the house is bound to do
something. He ought to hire a Punch and Judy
show, or get up a dance. This spice of bitterness
and flavour of rudeness was altogether characteristic
of Theresa, and somebody resented it by reminding
her that *she* was the hostess. "Of course," she
replied, "that is why I said it: what shall I do?"
One of her gifts was memory, and her friends cried
out at once that she should recite something. She
hesitated a little, and then throwing herself back in
her chair, began "*The Lass of Lochroyan.*" At first
she was rather diffident, but she gathered strength
as she went on. There is a passage in the middle of
the poem, in which Lord Gregory's cruel mother
pretends she is Lord Gregory, and refuses to recognise his former love, Annie of Lochroyan, as she
stands outside his tower. The mother calls to Annie
from the inside—

> "Gin thou be Annie of Lochroyan
>   (As I trow thou binna she),
> Now tell me some of the love tokèns
>   That passed between thee and me.

> "Oh dinna ye mind, Lord Gregory,
>   As we sat at the wine,

We changed the rings frae our fingers,
  And I can show thee thine?

"Oh yours was gude, and gude enough,
  But aye the best was mine;
For yours was o' the gude red gowd,
  But mine o' the diamond fine."

The last verse is as noble as anything in any ballad in the English language, and I thought that when Theresa was half way through it her voice shook a good deal. There was a glass of flowers standing near her, and just as she came to an end her arm moved and the glass was in a moment on the floor, shivered into twenty pieces. I happened to be watching her, and felt perfectly sure that the movement of her arm was not accidental, and that her intention was to conceal, by the apparent mishap, an emotion which was increasing and becoming inconvenient. At any rate, if that was her object it was perfectly accomplished, for the recitation was abruptly terminated, there was general commiseration over the shattered vase, and when the pieces were picked up and order was restored, it was nearly time to separate.

Two of my chief failings were forgetfulness and a want of thoroughness in investigation. What misery have I not suffered from insufficient presentation of a case to myself, and from prompt conviction of insufficiency and inaccuracy by the person to whom I in turn presented it! What misery have I not suffered from the discovery that explicit directions to me had been overlooked or only half understood! One day in particular, I had to take round a book to be "subscribed" which Wollaston had just published, that is to say, I had to take a copy to each of the leading booksellers to see how many they would purchase. Some books are sold "thirteen as twelve," the thirteenth book being given to the purchaser of twelve, and some are sold "twenty-five as twenty-four." This book was to be sold "twenty-five as twenty-four" according to Wollaston's orders. I subscribed it thirteen as twelve. Wollaston was annoyed, as I could see, for I had to go over all my work again, but in accordance with his fixed principles, he was not out of temper. It so happened that that same day he gave me some business correspondence which I was to look through; and having looked through it, I was to answer the last letter in the sense which he indicated. I read the correspondence and wrote the letter for his signature. As soon as he saw it, he pointed out to me that I had only half mastered the facts, and that my letter was all wrong. This greatly disturbed me, not only because I had vexed him and disappointed him, but because it was renewed evidence of my weakness. I thought that if I was incapable of getting to the bottom of such a very shallow complication as this, of what value were any of my thinkings on more difficult subjects, and I fell a prey to self-contempt and scepticism. Contempt from those about us is hard to bear, but God help the poor wretch who contemns himself. How well I recollect the early walk on the following morning in Kensington Gardens, the feeling of my own utter worthlessness, and the longing for death as the cancellation of the blunder of my existence! I went home, and after breakfast some proofs came from the printer of a pamphlet which Wollaston had in hand. Without unfastening them, he gave them to me, and said that as he had no time to read them himself, I must go upstairs to Theresa's study and read them off with her. Accordingly I went and began to read. She took the manuscript and I took the proof. She read about a page, and then she suddenly stopped. "O Mr. Rutherford," she said, "what have you done? I heard my uncle distinctly tell you to mark on the manuscript, when it went to the printer, that it was to be printed in demy octavo, and you have marked it twelvemo." I had had little sleep that night, I was exhausted with my early walk, and suddenly the room seemed to fade from me and I fainted. When I came to myself, I found that Theresa had not sought for any help; she had done all that ought to be done. She had unfastened my collar and had sponged my face with cold water. The first thing I saw as I gradually recovered myself, was her eyes looking steadily at me as she stood over me, and I felt her hand upon my head. When she was sure I was coming to myself, she held off and sat down in her chair. I was a little hysterical, and after the fit was over I broke loose. With a storm of tears, I laid open all my heart. I told her how nothing I had ever attempted had succeeded; that I had never even been able to attain that degree of satisfaction with myself and my own conclusions, without which a man cannot live; and that now I found I was useless, even to the best friends I had ever known, and that the meanest clerk in the city would serve them better than I did. I was beside myself, and I threw myself on my knees, burying my face in Theresa's lap and sobbing convulsively. She did not repel me, but she gently passed her fingers through my hair. Oh the transport of that touch! It was as if water had been poured on a burnt hand, or some miraculous Messiah had soothed the delirium of a fever-stricken sufferer, and replaced his visions of torment with dreams of Paradise. She gently lifted me up, and as I rose I saw her eyes too were

wet. "My poor friend," she said, "I cannot talk
to you now. You are not strong enough, and for
that matter nor am I, but let me say this to you,
that you are altogether mistaken about yourself.
The meanest clerk in the city could not take your
place here." There was just a slight emphasis I
thought upon the word "here." "Now," she said,
"you had better go. I will see about the pamphlet."
I went out mechanically, and I anticipate my story
so far as to say that, two days after, another proof came
in the proper form. I went to the printer to offer to
pay for setting it up afresh, and was told that Miss
Wollaston had been there and had paid herself for
the rectification of the mistake, giving special injunc-
tions that no notice of it was to be given to her
uncle. I should like to add one more beatitude
to those of the gospels and to say, Blessed are they
who heal us of self-despisings. Of all services
which can be done to man, I know of none more
precious.

When I went back to my work I worshipped
Theresa, and was entirely overcome with unhesitating
absorbing love for her. I saw nothing more of her
that day nor the next day. Her uncle told me that
she had gone into the country, and that probably
she would not return for some time, as she had
purposed paying a lengthened visit to a friend at a

distance. I had a mind to write to her; but I felt,
as I have often felt before in great crises, a restraint
which was gentle and incomprehensible, but nevertheless unmistakable. I suppose it is not what would
be called conscience, as conscience is supposed to
decide solely between right and wrong, but it was
none the less peremptory, although its voice was so
soft and low that it might easily have been overlooked. Over and over again, when I have purposed doing a thing, have I been impeded or arrested
by this same silent monitor, and never have I known
its warnings to be the mere false alarms of fancy.

After a time, the thought of Mary recurred to me.
I was distressed to find that, in the very height of
my love for Theresa, my love for Mary continued
unabated. Had it been otherwise, had my affection
for Mary grown dim, I should not have been so much
perplexed, but it did not. It may be ignominious
to confess it, but so it was; I simply record the fact.
I had not seen Mardon since that last memorable
evening at his house, but one day, as I was sitting
in the shop, who should walk in but Mary herself.
The meeting, although strange, was easily explained.
Her father was ill, and could do nothing but read.
Wollaston published freethinking books, and Mardon
had noticed in an advertisement the name of a book
which he particularly wished to see. Accordingly

he sent Mary for it. She pressed me very much to call on him. He had talked about me a good deal, and had written to me at the last address he knew, but the letter had been returned through the dead letter office. It was a week before I could go, and when I did go, I found him much worse than I had imagined him to be. There was no virulent disease of any particular organ, but he was slowly wasting away from atrophy, and he knew, or thought he knew, he should not recover. But he was perfectly self-possessed. "With regard to immortality," he said, " I never know what men mean by it. *What self is it which is to be immortal?* Is it really desired by anybody that he should continue to exist for ever with his present limitations and failings? Yet if these are not continued, the man does not continue, but something else, a totally different person. I believe in the survival of life and thought. People think that is not enough. They say they want the survival of their personality. It is very difficult to express any conjecture upon the matter, especially now when I am weak, and I have no system — nothing but surmises. One thing I am sure of, that a man ought to rid himself as much as possible of the miserable egotism which is so anxious about self, and should be more and more anxious about the Universal." Mardon grew slowly worse. The winter was coming on, and as the temperature fell, and the days grew darker, he declined. With all his heroism and hardness he had a weakness or two, and one was, that he did not want to die in London or be buried there. So we got him down to Sandgate near Hythe, and procured lodging for him close to the sea, so that he could lie in bed and watch the sun and moon rise over the water. Mary, of course, remained with him, and I returned to London. Towards the end of November I got a letter, to tell me that if I wished to see him alive again, I must go down at once. I went that day, and I found that the doctor had been, and had said that before the morning the end must come. Mardon was perfectly conscious, in no pain, and quite calm. He was just able to speak. When I went into his bedroom he smiled, and without any preface or introduction he said : " Learn not to be over-anxious about meeting troubles and solving difficulties which time will meet and solve for you." Excepting to ask for water, I don't think he spoke again. All that night Mary and I watched in that topmost garret looking out over the ocean. It was a night entirely unclouded, and the moon was at the full. Towards daybreak her father moaned a little, then became quite quiet, and just as the dawn was changing to sunrise, he passed away. What a sunrise it was! For about half an hour before the sun actually appeared, the perfectly smooth water was one mass of gently heaving opaline lustre. Not a sound was to be heard, and over in the south-east hung the planet Venus. Death was in the chamber, but the surpassing splendour of the pageant outside arrested us, and we sat awed and silent. Not till the first burning point of the great orb itself emerged above the horizon, not till the day awoke with its brightness and brought with it the sounds of the day and its cares, did we give way to our grief. It was impossible for me to stay. It was not that I was obliged to get back to my work in London, but I felt that Mary would far rather be alone, and that it would not be proper for me to remain. The woman of the house, in which the lodgings were, was very kind, and promised to do all that was necessary. It was arranged that I should come down again to the funeral. So I went back to London. Before I had got twenty miles on my journey the glory of a few hours before had turned into autumn storm. The rain came down in torrents, and the wind rushed across the country in great blasts, stripping the trees, and driving over the sky with hurricane speed great masses of continuous cloud, which mingled earth and heaven. I thought of all the ships which were on the sea in the night, sailing under the serene stars which I had seen rise and set; I thought of Mardon lying dead, and I thought of Mary. The simultaneous passage through great emotions welds souls, and begets the strongest of all forms of love. Those who have sobbed together over a dead friend, who have held one another's hands in that dread hour, feel a bond of sympathy, pure and sacred, which nothing can dissolve. I went to the funeral as appointed. There was some little difficulty about it, for Mary, who knew her father so well, was unconquerably reluctant that an inconsistency should crown the career of one who, all through life, had been so completely self-accordant. She could not bear that he should be buried with a ceremony which he despised, and she was altogether free from that weakness which induces a compliance with the rites of the Church from persons who avow themselves sceptics. At last a burying-ground was found, belonging to a little half-forsaken Unitarian chapel; and there Mardon was laid. A few friends came from London, one of whom had been a Unitarian minister, and he "conducted the service," such as it was. It was of the simplest kind. The body was taken to the side of the grave, and before it was lowered a few words were said, calling to mind all

the virtues of him whom we had lost. These the
speaker presented to us with much power and sympathy. He did not merely catalogue a disconnected
string of excellencies, but he seemed to plant himself
in the central point of Mardon's nature, and to see
from what it radiated. He then passed on to say
that about immortality, as usually understood, he
knew nothing; but that Mardon would live as every
force in nature lives—for ever; transmuted into a
thousand different forms; the original form utterly
forgotten, but never perishing. The cloud breaks up
and comes down upon the earth in showers which
cease, but the cloud and the showers are really
undying. This may be true, but, after all, I can only
accept the fact of death in silence, as we accept the
loss of youth and all other calamities. We are able
to see that the arrangements which we should make,
if we had the control of the universe, would be more
absurd than those which prevail now. We are able
to see that an eternity of life in one particular form,
with one particular set of relationships, would be
misery to many and mischievous to everybody;
however sweet those relationships may be to some
of us. At times we are reconciled to death as the
great regenerator, and we pine for escape from the
surroundings of which we have grown weary, but we
can say no more, and the hour of illumination has

not yet come.   Whether it ever will come to a more
nobly developed race, we cannot tell.

Thus far goes the manuscript which I have in my
possession.   I know that there is more of it, but all
my search for it has been in vain.   Possibly some
day I may be able to recover it.   My friend discontinued his notes for some years, and consequently
the concluding portion of them was entirely separate
from the earlier portion, and this is the reason, I
suppose, why it is missing.   Miss Mardon soon
followed her father.   She caught cold at his funeral ;
the seeds of consumption developed themselves with
remarkable rapidity, and in less than a month she
had gone.   Her father's peculiar habits had greatly
isolated him, and Miss Mardon had scarcely any
friends.   Rutherford went to see her continually, and
during the last few nights sat up with her, incurring
not a little scandal and gossip, to which he was
entirely insensible.   For a time he was utterly
broken-hearted ; and not only broken-hearted, but
broken-spirited, and incapable of attacking the least
difficulty.   All the springs of his nature were soft-
ened, so that if anything was cast upon him, there
it remained without hope, and without any effort
being made to remove it.   He only began to recover
when he was forced to give up work altogether and

take a long holiday. To do this he was obliged to
leave Mr. Wollaston, and the means of obtaining his
much-needed rest were afforded him, partly by what
he had saved, and partly by the kindness of one or
two whom he had known. I will just add what my
opinion of Rutherford was up to this point in his
life. He was emphatically the child of his time.
He was perpetually tormented by the presentation
of difficulties which he could not resolve, and he
could not put them on one side. The old order of
things had gone, and a new order of things had not
arisen. Unfortunately, too, for him, these difficulties
were not merely speculative, to be taken up and put
aside at pleasure. They haunted his whole existence, and prevented his enjoyment of it. The
thought of our mortality, of the cessation in vacancy
of the noblest men and women, preyed upon him
incessantly, and seemed to rob him of a good deal
of the natural interest which most men feel in
human affairs. So too with the thought of God. It
was his main business to wonder and despair over
it. He could not abandon it and say, " It does not
concern me," and yet he never obtained any certainty about it; nor could he ever in the least degree
reconcile what he thought he ought to believe about
God with the actual and apparently cruel facts of
nature. Again I say he was the child of his time, of

a time of transition, of a time when the earth under
our feet rocks and the foundations of everything are
shaken, of a time of intense misery to all those who
pine to be assured. I thought that Miss Mardon's
death would permanently increase my friend's intellectual despondency, but it did not. On the contrary, he gradually grew out of it. A crisis seemed
to take a turn just then, and he became less involved
in his old speculations, and more devoted to other
pursuits. I fancy that something happened; there
was some word revealed to him, or there was some
recoil, some healthy horror of eclipse in this self-
created gloom which drove him out of it. He
accidentally renewed his acquaintance with the
butterfly catcher, who was obliged to leave the
country and come up to London. He, however, did
not give up his old hobby, and the two friends used
every Sunday in summer time to sally forth some
distance from town and spend the whole live-long
day upon the downs and in the green lanes of
Surrey. Both of them had to work hard during the
week. Rutherford, who had learned shorthand when
he was young, got employment upon a newspaper,
and ultimately a seat in the gallery of the House of
Commons. He never took to collecting insects like
his companion, nor indeed to any scientific pursuits,
but he certainly changed. I find it very difficult to

describe exactly what the change was, because it was into nothing positive; into no sect, party, nor special mode. He did not, for example, go off into absolute denial. I remember his telling me, that to suppress speculation would be a violence done to our nation as unnatural as if we were to prohibit ourselves from looking up to the blue depths between the stars at night; as if we were to determine that nature required correcting in this respect, and that we ought to be so constructed as not to be able to see anything but the earth and what lies on it. Still, these things in a measure ceased to worry him, and the long conflict died away gradually into a peace not formally concluded, and with no specific stipulations, but nevertheless definitive. He was content to rest and wait. Better health and time, which does so much for us, brought this about. The passage of years gradually relaxed his anxiety about death by loosening his anxiety for life without loosening his love of life. But I would rather not go into any further details, because I still cherish the hope that some day or the other I may recover the contents of the diary. I am afraid that up to this point he has misrepresented himself, and that those who read his story will think him nothing but a mere egoist, selfish and self-absorbed. Morbid he may have been, but selfish he was not. A more perfect friend

I never knew, nor one more capable of complete abandonment to a person for whom he had any real regard, and I can only hope that it may be my good fortune to find the materials which will enable me to represent him autobiographically in a somewhat different light to that in which he appears now.

THE END.

PRINTED BY BALLANTYNE, HANSON AND CO.
EDINBURGH AND LONDON